ALL IN

The Bluegrass Story

MW01515238

To my Nigga
4-Trey! You ripped
me to the game now
I'm gone. Much Love

Ty a.k.a.
Topp Dawg

PFO-1 PRODUCTIONS

presents

ALL IN

The Bluegrass Story

By Tyrene "Topp Dawg" Collins

Published by
MIDNIGHT EXPRESS BOOKS

ALL IN

The Bluegrass Story

Copyright © 2012 by Tyrene "Topp Dawg" Collins

ISBN-10: 0985768673
ISBN-13: 978-0-9857686-7-6

Artwork by John Duckett

All rights reserved. No part of this book may be reproduced or transmitted in any form or by any means without written permission of the author.

Disclaimer: This is a work of fiction. All characters are totally from the imagination of the author and depict no persons, living or dead; any similarity is totally coincidental.

Published by
MIDNIGHT EXPRESS BOOKS
POBox 69
Berryville AR 72616
(870) 210-3772
MEBooks1@yahoo.com

PFO-1 PRODUCTIONS
presents

ALL IN
The Bluegrass Story

By Tyrene "Topp Dawg" Collins

ACKNOWLEDGMENTS

Yeah I know a lot of people are looking at this book with a look that says I wonder what's in it? Well I'll give you a little hint. A small city/country boy who has been in and out of prison his whole adult life. But I did something different this time beside lift weights and watch sports. I put my heart in this book. I hope all who reads this book enjoy it cause part two will set the city on fire. That's right I'll be right back at ya'll!'

MOMMA- I did it! Something positive for all to enjoy. But I want everybody to know you're the only woman in my life who never turned her back on me. Right or wrong you're standing next to me. I know I don't have to say thanks cause that's what moms are suppose to do but thanks from the bottom of my heart. You're the sun that makes my dark world so bright. I love you like you love me UNCONDITIONALLY!!!

TO MY BROTHER AND SISTERS- All ya'll have been holding me down and that means the world to me. I know it ain't been easy watching me run in and out of these hell hole's but ya'll be right there to help break my fall.

CHARLENE- I know you have been gone for some time now, but I think of you often. It took me some time to adjust to doing time without you but I found out that you were still in my HEART.

FAMILY- To the few who actually care, thanks for the support and love you send my way. For the rest, I thought I would let you know I'm still standing and doing just fine.

ALAYSHA AND JAH QUEZ- Ya'll not old enough to read this book yet but know I did it with both of you on my mind.

Alaysha you told me something when you were a little girl that stuck on my heart until now. You said you wasn't going to love nobody else cause everybody you loved went to jail. Well baby girl I'm here to tell you don't be afraid to love cause love will find its way back to you.

Jah Quez- GRADES FIRST! One in 100,000 young men go pro in any sport. I would love nothing better than for you to be that one. But we're not going to bet on that long shot so we're going to put all our eggs on EDUCATION a sure bet.

REAL NIGGAS- PLEASE STAND UP TO THE OVATION YOU DESERVE!

ALL MY DAWGS around the world, I'm standing on that! PDL, 456, IFGB, Mafia, APB, Villains, Bounty Hunters, Queen St., all the Piru's, Outlaw 20's, BPS, Brims, Swans and all my West Coast. All my niggas on the East Coast standing on all fours like a real DAWG ROOF ROOF MUTHA FUCKA!!!

I didn't forget about home and my niggas from all over the state of KENTUCKY. All my LEXINGTON niggas who showed love on the streets and in the pen; much love.

My LOUISVILLE niggas that I know ya'll alwayz had a niggas back THANKS. My niggas from the 148(PARIS) fresh out of prison ya'll put a nigga on his feet. (Black) we knew GEORGETOWN and PARIS didn't get along but we made it work THANKS! To all the real niggas around the BLUEGRASS who I've had the pleasure of knowing and doing business with please stand tall cause we're a factor in any game we play in.

One more thing before I go. I ain't mad or bitter; it's all part of this game we play. I had my run as The King of the City and it was one helluva run.

MOTTO I LIVE BY:

IF IT'S FUCK ME, YOU KNOW IT'S FUCK YOU!!!

CHAPTER 1

August, 1996 in the small city of Georgetown, Kentucky

"Damn, Bugz. Why you alwayz rolling up those mutha fuckin seeds?"

Now, Bugz has been my main man since fat crayons and car seats. So no matter what it is it's on, when we're together, my name is Dawg. When we're not in some shit, I go to school everyday. I'm not a book worm, but I play football and basketball so that's enough to keep me coming back; plus my girl Faye. But right now, we're on same *get paid type shit* so everything else takes a backseat to what's about to go down.

"Nigga, quit crying; this all we got right now. After we handle this business, we'll get same of that (Elvis)."

I know he's right but damn, my nerves are all on edge cause anything can happen when the211 game was in progress.

"Bust this right the spot up here on the left."

I pulled over at the E-Z Way Mart a few doors down from the Same As Pay Check Exchange.

"Look, my nigga; it's some nice paper up in this bitch so be alive and bust anybody who's out of place."

As I looked over at my man Bugz, I saw him talking but I couldn't hear a word coming out of his mouth. The look I saw on his face before he pulled down his Jason mask; shit about to go down. I hope we don't have to leave no bodies up in this bitch.

Across Town at the high school.........

"Girl, you know Bugz be having Telly (yeah that's my real name) out there on that bullshit!"

That's big mouth Cee-Cee all in my business. Her and Faye been cool since grade school so she calls herself looking out for her.

"You know what I have seen him with a lot of money and new clothes lately. I'm going to ask him about it later."

"You need to, cause he got a chance to get up out of the hood and make something of himself."

"Let me worry about that let's just get ready for track practice."

Meanwhile, back on the other side of town...

"Bitch don't move; I want everybody over there by that desk now!"

While Bugz had everybody at bay with that SKS assault rifle, I was behind the counter getting all the cake.

"Make sure you don't leave these rotting mutha fucka's one penny in this bitch."

You know those check cashing places be taxing the every day worker, so we putting the tax down on they punk ass.

"Let's roll baby boy; it's a wrap up in this mutha fucka."

"Everybody down on the floor and start counting from 100 down to 1."

With everybody on the floor, we walked out of the store and hopped in my murder bucket (my 68 Delta 88). As we're pulling out of the parking, lot I see Robbery/Homicide Detective Chris Palmer pulling in the E-Z

Way Mart. He waves at me, but when he looks across the seat and sees my man Bugz, his smile turns upside down.

"Dawg, fuck that pussy-ass nigga; if I ever get a chance, I'm going to put one in that nigga head."

"Yeah, whatevea. Where you going? I got to go to football practice."

"Take me to Goldie's house; we're going to smoke and play the new Madden."

"That's cool. Count the money and split it so I know what we got."

While I'm driving, my mind is on why do I keep doing this shit when I got a nice bank roll stashed at my granny's house over on TeddyAvenue

"Damn dawg; we must caught than sucker with all the money up front."

"What did you just say?"

"You heard me. Shit was real sweet; we got $13,500 a piece."

"Damn that little hole in the wall had that much cake up in there?"

"Bout to buy me a nice ride and put some rims on that bitch."

"Nigga be easy with that money; people already talking shit about us."

"Why the fuck you alwayz worried about what people say? I don't give a fuck when it comes to getting money. Besides, you keep playing like you do on Friday night and get a major school to offer you a full ride; I know you're going to play on Sundays."

"I just don't want you to blow your money and be crying to me when you're broke."

"Fuck that! When I'm broke, I'm going to use Doll Baby to get some money." (Doll Baby is his SKS Assault Rifle)

"Yeah I'm with you all the way but I've been saving my money so we can buy a couple of thangs."

"Fuck that shit; we'll rob them pussy-niggas, too."

"Nah, we going to let them live cause the state and feds are hot on most of them niggas ass anyway."

"If you say so, but peep this - what's up for later tonight?"

"Me and Faye going to the movies and to get something to eat."

"Pussy-whupped-ass nigga; let that country bitch go. Let's go holla at same of the home girls from Northern Heights."

"Nigga, watch yo mouth. You and Goldie go holla at them hood ratz. I'll get with you later."

"Stay up my nigga; I'll get at you."

"Tell Goldie I said what's up and ya'll fools don't miss my game Friday night."

"We won't much love my nigga."

As I watch my man get out the car Goldie was already standing in the front door throwing up the set I know now why I keep putting the 211 game into play. Shit real sweet and it's my first love.

Later that night........

"Damn baby girl; you been real quiet all night. What's on your mind?"

"I got something to asks you and don't lie to me, Telly."

When she uses my real name, shit about to get deep. I hope she didn't find out about me fucking with that white girl Amanda.

"You know I'm going to keep it gangster with you, baby girl."

"Well word around school and the streetz are you and Bugz are robbing everything around town and in Paris and Lexington."

This had to have come from Goldie running his mouth. We took his ass with us on a couple of the licks and I'll be damn if it ain't biting me in the ass. He's getting high with them bitches and been pillow-talking going to get all us a L-Bow (life sentence).

"Nah baby, that shit ain't true; why you listening to everybody talking anyway?"

"That's just it, Telly; everybody talking bout ya'll and how they alwayz see the murder bucket parked in some weird places."

Those mutha fuckas are nosey probably seen us parked checking one of those spots we be jacking. I can't tell her me and my man been on an all out robbing spree. Hell, she ain't ready for that so I do what I know best for her - I lie.

"You know it was probably broke down when those people saw it were it was at."

The look she gave me let me know she knew I was lying cause she knew the motor in the murder bucket was super tight. That bitch would make it to Cali and back without a problem.

"Well, what are you doing to make your money? I know your Uncle Steve's lawn care service don't pay you that much."

"Fuck it; I can't lie to you. I've been hustling a few rocks over in the projects, nothing major just to get some extra ends."

"A few rocks my ass. This is a brand new 96' Super Sport Impala, plus you stay fresh to death with all the new J's."

"Yeah, the clothes and shit came from my granny when she be winning at the track plus my moms be looking out like a mutha fucka, too."

"What about the car, Telly?"

"My older sister Simone got good credit you can get anything you want with that shit."

"I'm just scared; I don't want to lose you over no stupid shit."

"You won't, baby girl."

That was all I could say cause I don't never know when our luck is going to run out.

"So, what we about to do."

"What time you got to be home anyway, Faye?"

"I don't. I told my granny I was staying over at Cee-Cee's house so the ball in your court, baby."

Damn what good luck my granny is at the bingo hall so I can sneak ole girl upstairs before she gets home cause she'll be up all night watching TVG horse racing – that's where you can call and make bets right from your own living room."

"Ain't no thang on my end; ain't nobody home but my little cousin L-Boogie; his bad ass probably playing that damn Dream Cast."

"Let's do it then, baby. I hate riding around town so late I feel like everybody watching me gives me the creeps."

"Don' trip, baby. You're with the prince of the city, plus we're in my hood so shit straight."

"Okay, baby; I love you."

"'Love you, baby girl."

Just liked I figured my little cousin was up playing that damn Dream Cast. Don't know why I brought him a Play Station.

"What's up, L?"

"Ain't nothing Dawg. Granny said make sure you pick her up at 1:00 a.m."

"True, but why don't she ride with Ms. Josephine?"

"I don't know, just make sure we ain't late cause I don't want to hear her bitching at us."

"I dig it, fam; we'll be on time."

"What's up Faye?"

"Ain't nothing cutie pie."

She leaned over and kissed him on his face. That little nigga turned beet red when she did that. L's getting on up in age (12) so you know his little dick be getting hard.

"Faye, why you do that? You know I got a girl friend now."

"Boy shut up I've been kissing you on your little dirty face for 3 years now."

"That's what my woman for ain't that right Dawg?"

I just throw my hands up in the air cause I know she's about to have some fun with his young ass.

"Little nigga your girl ain't built like this."

I can't lie Faye was straight ass muttha fucka. Nice titties, a six-pack, cause she was on the track team so you know she stayed in shape, and a fat ole ass. Damn, I can't wait to get her upstairs.

"Yo. Ya'll quit the bull shitting. Faye get yo ass upstairs so I can go get Granny; it's 12:45 a.m. and you know she's going to show off if she stands outside one minute."

"Yeah, you right, baby; tell Bell I said hello."

"Tell her yoself cause you know she's coming upstairs like she does every night."

"But I'm alwayz in the closet; remember, baby?"

"Yeah, your right. But look baby, you can take a shower now or when I get back we'll get in there together."

"I'll wait on you baby just hurry up and get back; I hate it up here by myself."

"I will baby. Let's roll L cause if I don't bring you Bell going to trip!"

"Yeah, let's roll fam so Bell won't be standing outside with all that money!"

A few blocks over in Northern Heights housing projects…

My man Bugz and Goldie got two girls from over that way. Kay and Ken are from over there so I know them niggas are strapped like they on their way to war. I wouldn't have it no other way for me and my niggas cause we be in all kinds of shit. Shoot first asks questions later.

"Goldie, roll up same of that good shit."

"Damn nigga, we done smoked up half the zip already my mutha fucking chest feels like it's about to bust wide open."

My nigga Bugz is a jet-black, slim nigga with a look in his eyes that the whole world would know he's a stone cold killa.

"Nigga, I tell you what keep yo dry ass lipz off my shit when I do twist it up."

"Yeah whatevea, nigga. I'm going to step outside for a minute."

At the bingo hall...

As I pull up to the hall my little cousin was zoned out listening to C-Bo. Man this nigga talking bout cooking up work hoping the Federally don't raid cause all a nigga want to do is get paid. Damn I wanted to get paid, too. The D-Boyz around my way was getting real nice paper, so I was going to holla at Fat Man when I got my paper right.

"L, go open the door for Bell like a real playa."

That little nigga loved that old lady with all his heart. As I watched my granny come out the hall, she rubbed L on the head and he smiled from ear to ear. Bell's a short woman and a little chubby but her hair is jet black and alwayz curled. L opened the back door for Bell to get in.

"Hey old bird, did you win some money up in there tonight?"

"Old bird my ass boy! Don't make me put my foot up in yo skinny little ass."

I smiled cause she smelled like a million cigarettes and she don't even smoke.

"Yeah, I knocked them fools for about $1700 and I hit for $3000 today at the race track."

"Can I hold a few dollars since you hit them like that."

She rolled her eyes cause she knew my pocket stays fat.

"L, you want something to eat baby?"

"Nah Bell, I'm cool but you know school starts next week and the new J's came out today."

I knew without a doubt those J's were as good as brought. Wouldn't nothing Bell wouldn't do in her power to make that little boy happy.

"Baby, you know if I'm able, the world is yours, so the shoes ain't no thing. Telly, take him with you when you go in the morning to get yo shoes cause I know you and Little Henry are going straight to the mall anyway."

"I got him Bell."

Back in the Heights…

As Goldie stepped out on the front porch, what he saw made his blood boil. Some dumb ass nigga from over there was bent over in his trunk. He got major knock in his 442 Oldsmobile. Good thing the porch light wasn't on so that nigga never saw him coming over to his car. Bugz came out of the house and didn't see Goldie on the front porch. He hollas for him. Damn, he saved that dumb ass nigga's life when he did that. That fool looked up just in time to hear those big ass bees fly by his head. That nigga must be kin to Carl Lewis cause that nigga got ghost.

"Damn!" That was Goldie talking to himself as he closed his trunk.

"Damn nigga, who you popping at?" Bugz asked as he ran over with his 17-shot Glock in his hand.

"I don't know nigga! If you don't be hollering and screaming like some broad, I would have pushed that nigga's wig back."

"Yeah whatevea; let's raise up out this bitch before 5-0 start rolling."

"What about ole girl'em?"

"Nigga, fuck them bitches; we'll get at them on a later date."

"No bullshit; I hear than people coming now!!!"

Over on Teddy Avenue, 1:30 a.m...

As Bell walked in the house, she did her regular routine cutting on every downstairs light. I shot straight up the stairs before she could start about school and shit. Bell is real big on grades, but not tonight; I got Faye up here and shit bout to be on. When I got to my room, all the light were out.

"Baby, you sleep?"

"Nah baby; waiting on you to get back."

"Okay, I'm bout to hit the shower; you straight or what?"

"Nigga, I told you I was waiting for you so let's go cause I want you right now."

Man, she wasn't playing cause when she passed me, she was butt naked. I fell in behind her so Bell wouldn't hear all those foot steps up here. As I closed the door to the bathroom I couldn't keep my eyes off of her. With the water running she stepped in and left the curtain open so I can see her getting wet. Damn, I couldn't get out my clothes fast enough. By the time I did get in with her, my dick was standing straight out in front of me.

"Damn baby, you happy to see me or what?"

"You know I can't help myself when it comes to you."

"If that's the case let me help you with your problem, baby."

Then, without another word, she drops to her knees and put me right in her mouth. Damn, I had to brace myself by putting my hands out on the wall to keep from falling over. After a few minutes of that good head she stood up and put one foot up on the side of the tub and bent over while looking over her shoulder.

"Give it to me, baby; please."

"Only if you call me Daddy."

"Please, Daddy."

When I slid up in that pussy, I almost busted right then. It was so hot and tight in there, I felt like I couldn't breath." "Damn baby, this pussy is a good-ass mutha fucka."

"Oooh baby, fuck me."

Hearing those words made me speed up and act a fool in that pussy.

"Ooooh baby, I'm bout to cum."

"Yeah baby; do that shit."

As she was cumming all over me shaking and with a low moan a few strokes, later I pulled out and shot off all over her pretty ass. We finished our shower and headed back to my room. On my way, I looked in L's room - he had the door open cause ain't no air in our projects. I know he saw Faye wrapped up in that towel.'

"L, you straight, fam."

"Yeah, I'm cool; don't forget I'm rolling with you in a couple of hours to the mall."

"You know I wouldn't forget you for the world, plus what Bell says is law with us."

"Sho you right fam; sho you right."

As I'm about to turn and head to my room, L throws up the set all I can do is hit'em back up that's my little nigga right there."

Chapter 2

The next morning at Bell's...

A few hours later I was up moving around in my room trying to be quiet so I didn't wake Faye. I grabbed a pair of polo jeans, a red t-shirt and red chucks and walked down the hall to L's room. When I got there, that little nigga was dressed and counting his money me and Bell give him.

"What's up, fam?"

"Shit little nigga, have you been to sleep yet?"

"Just like you, all I need is a few hours of sleep."

"What you doing with all that paper?"

"Going to buy the matching sweat suit to go with the new J's."

"Give me a few minutes to get myself together then we'll roll out."

After I got dressed, I went back in my room to check on Faye' to my surprise she was awake.

"Hey baby, you okay?"

"Why wouldn't I be, I'm with you remember."

"That's what's up baby; you want something from the mall?"

"Nah baby, but give me some money so I can go see Ms. Winky and get my hair done since you messed it up lasted night."

All I could do was smile remembering that episode in the shower last night so I got no problem getting her hair done. "Here's enough to get your nails and toes done, too."

"Thanks baby, I love you."

"I know, I love you too."

Downstairs…

That young boy thinks he's slick like I don't know what going on in my own house. Well, this morning I got something for his slick ass.

"Morning Bell."

"Hey grandson, where's that baby boy?"

"On his way down now. What smells good, granny?"

"Just a little breakfast so ya'll come on and eat so ya'll can go."

Damn, I was trying to get out the door so Bell would do what she does every day after 7:00 a.m. she goes to the Sunoco to get the local paper, lottery tickets, and the daily racing form. That way Faye could sneak out and lock up behind herself; she's got keys to the house and to my 96' Impala.

"Nah Bell, we got to roll so we can get there before the line gets too long."

"Boy you got time to sit down and have breakfast with an old lady."

"When I call you an old lady you be ready to bust my head."

"Cause boy I say what I want and you say what I tell you to." With a little smirk on her face, she made her last statement I know something was about to hit the fan, I just can't put it together.

"Nah, Bell we really got to roll."

"All right. Since my grandsons can't have breakfast with me, tell that girl upstairs to come eat with me then."

Damn I said to myself; I can't get shit pass Bell; she's brown paper news (means she knows everything).

"Ma'am."

"Don't ma'am me and go tell that girl I said came on down here."

I guess Faye heard what was going on cause I heard her coming down the steps.

"Morning, Ms. Jenny Bell."

"And good morning to you Faye you hungry, baby; I know this fool ain't got enough sense to feed you?"

"Yes, ma'am."

I know Bell. She's about to give us the business, so L grabs his plate and heads to the table. Me, I just stand by and wait.

"Faye, your granny know you stayed over here last night?"

"No, ma'am."

"Well, you and Telly ain't grown."

"I know Bell; I'm sorry."

"Don't be sorry, be careful. Both of ya'll got a chance to make it."

"I love him Bell; can't stand not being around him as much as I can."

"Don't let love make you stupid cause that boy has that affect on everybody. He'll be going away to school next year; who knows where he's going?"

"He told me maybe Cincinnati or Western Kentucky."

"Baby girl, don't get your hopes too high; that boy wants to see the world."

"I guess you're right, Bell."

"Let him become a man; if ya'll's love is true, it will work itself out."

"All right, Bell."

"Okay baby, let's eat so these fools can get the hell out my house."

Out the door to the mall...

As me and L walked out the front door, my man Bugz was sitting on the back of the murder bucket. That shit creeps me out sometimes. That nigga alwayz popping up out of nowhere; like he's my body guard or something.

"Damn nigga, what you been doing standing out here all night or some shit?"

"Nigga, my old man dropped me over here on his way to work. Bitching bout me getting a job."

"Yeah, a job and a pad so I can crash over there."

"Damn that does sound good; I'm going to look into that real soon."

"Yeah, you do that; my nigga, that would be real sweet."

"What's up L? What you doing up this early trying to roll with the big dawgs?"

"Ain't nothing; just trying to get the new J's. Plus being from the North makes you a big dawg anyway."

That put a smile on me and Bugz face cause he's right being from the North is what it's all about not only that what street your from. Me, I'm from Teddy Avenue, Bugz was from Booker T. Much love to all my niggas from Main Avenue, Chambers Avenue, West Lynn, Brown St. Payne Avenue West St. and the whole Black Bottom

Across town at the police precinct…

Detective Palmer and his punk-ass hillbilly partner Detective Reeves had been putting niggas from the North in jail for years. O.G niggas like O, Turtle, my Uncle A.T and a few of the homies they turned over to the Feds. What makes shit so bad was Detective Palmer was right from Main Avenue on the far end were it meets with Brown Street.

"I'm so sick of all these fucking robberies going on all over the city; I know it's that little bastard from over on the North side."

"Chris, calm your nerves. I know you want to solve these cases but don't get all worked up over nothing. Plus high school football kicks off next Friday and we're ranked #2 behind the defending state 6A champs, Louisville St. X."

"Yeah, that's reminds me; I seen that all-state strong safety the other day pulling out the E-Z Way Mart parking lot."

"Now talking about a true ball hawk, that kid was all over the field last year; he had 12 interceptions and 6 punt returns for touchdowns."

"Yeah, that's all good Gary but I seen him with Henry Lewis, a.k.a Bugz."

That cracker turned beet red when he heard my man's name. Some wild shit happened a few years back when Bugz was into stealing cars. See, one night at the Super 8 Motel, Bugz stole a 92' Camry to joy ride in but to his surprise, the car he took was Detective Reeves' wife's car. She was at the motel with one of my home boys from the hood. So the police pulled Bugz over in the car, ran the tags on the car and they came back to Angie Reeves. The officers looked at each other and went to radio the detective. By the time he got to the scene, one of the patrol men had called his cell phone and told him what Bugz had said.

"Now, I'm going to ask you again; where the hell did you get my wife's car?"

"I told you once, the Super 8 Motel!"

"I don't believe you but if you're lying, I'm going to break your little nigger neck."

"Don't be mad at me cause yo wife a tramp-bitch."

Pow was all you heard when the detective slapped the shit out of my man while he was cuffed. The smile that spread across my man Bugz face would have sent chill bumps down Super Man's back. "One day you'll regret putting your hands on me."

"Well, it won't be today you little black monkey. Officer, take this stupid mutha fucka to Cisco Road."

That's a juvenile jail in Lexington that houses youthful offenders from all over the state. Just so happened, we're only 14 miles away.

On his way to the motel, the detective had a million-and-one questions why his wife's car would be at the motel. Once there he and another officer went to the front desk.

"May I help you, sir?"

"Yes, you can. Do you have an Angie Reeves as a guest?"

"I can't give you that kind of information, sir."

"Oh, but its police business." Detective Reeves said as he flashed his badge and while the other officer looked around.

"Okay, hold on one second. Room 145 down the hall on the end."

"Would you have an extra key to that room?"

"Here you go, sir; be careful."

"Thanks young lady; we will."

By the time they got to the room they were looking for, you could hear all kinds of moaning and groaning. The officer with him didn't pull his gun out like the detective did cause he knew what was going on behind that closed door. Detective Reeves slipped the key in the lock and slid right in with the other officer right behind him without any one noticing them.

What he saw made his stomach turn-upside-down. His pretty little wife with Big Country dick all in her mouth. With the show still going on, the young officer with Detective Reeves was growing a tent in his pants and what he saw next, made him want to try the detective's wife himself.

He heard Country say, "I'm cumming bitch!"

All she did was suck it harder. Her eyes finally landed on her husband but that didn't stop her from sucking on Country until his dick went soft in her mouth. Tramp bitch just like Bugz said.

"What the fuck is he doing with that numb nuts?"

"They'd been running together since they were kids over on Teddy Avenue and Booker T. plus Shawn Garrett, a.k.a Goldie, runs with them."

"Sometimes the bank and check-cashing people said it was three suspects; sometimes two."

"He's got a chance of a life time; you think he's running with those clowns?"

"He might, you just keep an eye on him and see what he's up too. Damn, I hope he don't fuck up the run at the state title."

"I followed him lasted night with that pretty, little young girl from the country. But all they did was go to the movie and to get something to eat. After that, he went home."

"Well somebody doing it; we need to find out who."

"Yes we do partner, yes do."

Meanwhile, at the mall, 8:15 a.m…

"Damn it's packed in here to get these mutha fucking J's."

"Dawg, you think your man is going to be able to get us straight?"

"Yeah, he should cause I dropped an extra $50 on each pair every time we come."

The way it looked, shit might be tight when we get up here. Damn, just when I had a little hope for us getting the shoes, shit got real tight when I saw them niggas from the East Side of Lexington. A whole bunch of them carrying Foot Locker bags. I seen a few of them niggas at a couple of games last year when we played the city schools."

As they passed us, the real black nigga of the crew said "Aye country nigga, that's why Dunbar's going to kick ya'll ass in three weeks!"

"Peep this family be at the game in a few weeks and I'll bring you the football after I return a punt."

"Country nigga, I'll give you $500 every time you bring me the ball."

"Make sure your bank roll is tight cause I'll be seeing you a whole lot."

"You must don't know my bank is alwayz tight, country nigga."

"Sho you right."

We kept it pushing on our way to the Foot Locker and the line was super stupid niggas and bitches everywhere.

"Ya'll stay right here I'm going to the front and see what's up."

"Okay my nigga; bark if you me

"L, what size you want in case I see my dude while I'm up here?"

"9 fam and a XL sweat suit."

"I need a 10 ½, Dawg."

"Nigga I know what size you wear fool, as many a times we been up here on the same mission."

That nigga just smiled as I made my way to the front. I was getting a few mean mugs from the niggas and a few whispers from the ladies. I was almost to the front when my dude saw me.

"Country ass Georgetown nigga, where the hell you been at?"

"What's up Bye my nigga?"

"You damn near got yo shoes sold to these niggas."

I turned around and all I saw was niggas from my hood: Mailman, T-Parker and Pretty Toni.

"Is that right."

"I got enough for them niggas but yo boy wants two pairs of 10 1/2."

"Damn Toni you alwayz trying to buy everything so the next nigga can't shine."

"You know me Dawg, I just want a pair for later."

"Yeah I can dig it, but you know Bugz needs a 10½."

"Dig, where that nigga at anyway?"

"Back there with L probably trying to put his bullshit mack down on them girls."

This nigga Pretty Toni is from West Lynn. He's a young nigga like me but he's getting that rock money and shit looks like he's really getting it.

"Mailman, what's up my nigga?"

"Ain't nothing, just trying to get these shoes for me and the kids."

"Damn nigga, you do that and won't be no more shoes in the store."

This nigga breaks down in his boxing stance like he's ready to swing on me. That niggas' hands are real good.

"Parker, you ready for school, my nigga?"

"Yeah, we just got back from the Memphis Steam Boat Classic."

"Yeah, wish I could've gone but football practice comes first right now."

"We know we'll be waiting on you when the season is over."

That nigga is a basketball star, sho nuff; that young nigga was the only freshman on the varsity team last year. Got plenty of clock playing with my nigga J.T. who's down at Saint Katherine's College playing ball this year.

"Cool baby boy; you straight on getting your shoes and shit?"

"Yeah, Dawg; I got enough."

"All right ya'll be easy and I'll see ya'll at the block party tonight."

This was the end of the summer and the back to school party be off the hook. Niggas who don't even go to school be there; honeys everywhere.

"Yo Bye, you ready for me yet?"

"Yeah my nigga shit's ready."

"That's what's up, but let me holla at you bout something."

"Yeah what's on yo mind country boy?"

"Those East Side niggas were just up here and as they passed us one of them niggas said some slick shit to me."

"What he say and which one was it?"

"The dark, heavy set one, that nigga said Dunbar was going to kick are ass."

"You know ya'll going to get ya'll ass kicked by all the city school."

"We'll see but I told that nigga be at the game cause I was going to bring him the ball when I return a punt said he would give me $500 every time I brought him the ball."

"Well nigga, make sure you take that nigga the ball then."

"That's what was on my mind is that niggas money, right?"

"What you don't know you talking bout Von that nigga getting real money all than East Side niggas getting paper."

"Cool, you make sure you're at the game and I'll put on a show for you."

"I wouldn't miss it for the world with ya'll being #2(Scott County) and (Dunbar) being #5 that is going to set the tone for the whole season."

"True but I'm bout to break up out of here thanks for the love and information."

"No doubt; see ya'll in two months when the red and white 13 came out."

"You know you will."

"One."

Yeah one love."

On my way back to get with Bugz and L, somebody grabbed my hand so I turned to see who got their hands all over me. "Damn baby girl, you know me or something?"

"Nah but, I might be trying too."

"The way you got yo hands on me, you're past trying; what's your name?"

"Janelle."

"Janelle!"

"Yeah, that's my name."

I can't lie. Baby girl was looking real good in her cheerleading shorts and flip flops with that tight ass Tates Creek t-shirt on.

"I'm Dawg."

"That's it, Dawg. I know yo mamma didn't name you that."

"Well if you want to know my real name I play football for Scott County and we play Tates Creek in November so you be there and you'll hear my name over the loud speaker."

"I might be there."

"Well, if you ain't you'll be missing the only star in the city that night."

"Star. Huh? We'll see."

"Well, baby girl, nice meeting you but I got to roll; hope to see you again one day."

"You just might see me sooner then you think."

On my way over to Bugz and L who were looking at jewelry in the middle of the mall. Them Arabs nigga alwayz trying to sell a young nigga that shit. How can they sell a $5000 chain for $1800; you do the math.

"Dawg, you like this chain?"

"Let me see it, turn around."

Shit did look good on my black-ass partner but I know the diamonds are cloudy ass a mutha fucka.

"If you like it my nigga, get it so we can roll out."

"Dawg, who's that bad bitch you was talking to?"

"Some chick who goes to Tates Creek trying to be fresh with a nigga."

"Her ass is fat as a mutha fucka."

As me and L turned to look one more time, her and her friends were walking past us smiling and waving. Boy, all them broads were bad.

"Ooh, we fam!"

"I feel you, baby boy; I feel you.!!

"I'm ready. My nigga shit hit me for $2200 but ain't no thang."

"Do you my nigga; do you?"

"Can't wait til the party jumps off tonight."

"Dawg, you going to ask Bell if I can go down the street to the party with you?"

"You know she's going to let you go, school starts Monday and you'll be with me. So be easy and ready to roll at about 9:00 p.m.

The block party – what a way to end the summer…

As I'm getting dressed L knocks on my door for the tenth time asking, "Are you ready yet?"

"Them little tackhead girls you and Don-Don be chasing after ain't going nowhere."

"Nah, fam. You said 9:00 and it's 10:30 and I can hear the music way up here."

"Here I come; just one more thing little nigga."

I sprayed my cool water on and told him to come and get a little bit behind his ear so the young girls would be all over him. Plus, I tucked my

.38 snub-nose in my back pocket; nothing too big but enough to make a nigga act right.

As we headed out my room, L was behind me. I turned and asked him, "Can you see my gun?"

"Nah, your t-shirt got it covered."

"Good cause I know Bell's up."

Just as I thought, when we got to the bottom of the stairs, she was sitting in her chair watching Fox 56 local news.

"Ya'll be careful down there."

"Yes ma'am."

"L, you get back here before 12:00 a.m."

"But Bell, it's almost 11:00 p.m. now."

"Okay 1:00 a.m. and not one minute later, you understand me boy?"

"Yes ma'am."

"Later, Bell."

"I love ya'll boy's."

"We know."

Out the door and as soon as we closed the door, we saw my man standing by the bucket.

"It took ya'll long enough."

"You know that nigga Bugz in there trying to be all pretty and shit."

"That's why all the girls love me."

Just as Bugz was about to say some slick shit, the front door opened and Bell was standing at the screen door. She said, "Don't be down there acting no fool you and little Henry cause if you do you know, I'll know before you get home. Mrs. Mary will be looking."

"We ain't, Bell; we'll be cool."

"An boy, tighten that belt up; that gun's got your pants hanging all off yo ass." Then Bell closed the door.

"Bell don't miss shit, Dawg."

"Who you telling?"

"Let's go ya'll; I ain't got all night like you two fools."

"Damn little nigga, we ready and don't get down here acting like no mark either."

"Nigga I'm from Teddy Avenue; fool ain't no marks over here."

We made our way down the street and around the corner when we saw what every young nigga wants to see when it's a party - people everywhere; all ages, even some white kids. Man niggas got they cars parked all out in the middle of the street; rims shining. L breaks as soon as he sees our cousin Don-Don.

"Yo, L. Meet me down on the corner of Teddy and West Lynn at 12:50 a.m. little nigga."

"All right fam, I hear you."

"Don't make Bell come down here looking for yo ass."

"I won't cause I know she going to act a donkey."

"Be easy and watch what you're doing."

But I spoke too late; my words fell on deaf ears cause that nigga was half way across the park.

Me and Bugz made our way up the street to Snoop's house. I know this nigga got a yard full. On our way I see Pretty Toni's 86' regal with hydraulics parked on 3-wheel motion in front of Mrs. Mary house; that's his granny. As we got to Snoop's house them niggas had a dice game jumping like a mutha fucka. All the niggas from the hood was in a big-ass circle: Darnell, Mailman, Pooh, Disco, DMack, Boo, Melvin, my brother Scoobie, Jim-Bob, J.P., G Wayne, Burger, Big Hurt, J.D., Lil Wayne(from Zionhill), Red, Saint, Bay Bay, Pretty Toni, Charlie Boy, Fat Man, Monte, Thunder, Oh Rock, and Crusher Day. Something was bound to happen with all them wild-ass niggas gambling and drinking.

"What's up ya'll?"

All them fool-ass niggas raised up from the game.

"Baby bruh, what's up? Ready for next Friday?"

"Hell yeah, oh before I forget to tell you, I'm wearing number 2 this year."

That put a smile on his face cause that nigga was a bad mutha fucka on that field a couple of years ago.

"That's cool baby boy; but make sure you wear it right."

"I got you, big bruh."

A few more niggas pop slick but bull shitting all at the same time so we made our way around back to get with Snoop. That nigga was on the back porch with them dark-ass sunglasses on and it's dark as mutha fucka back here.

31

"What's up, young niggas?"

We answer together, "You got it."

"Get one of those cold beers out the cooler Dawg; no smoke for you the season getting ready to start."

"I already took my physical about a month ago."

"Well so what? I want you with a clear mind on that field, so lay off that shit until the season is over."

"More like the whole school year; you forgot I play basketball, too."

"Damn I sho didn't; ya'll got ya'll's asses ran off the court at the Sweet Sixteen last year by Breckenridge County."

"Them fools won the state title, don't forget."

"Sho did baby boy, but look what's up with you and Jesse James right here?"

"What you mean by that, my nigga?"

"Word on the streets is you two little niggas been putting in same major work."

I know I could lie to this nigga and put the spin game on him but this nigga knows everything plus I might need him with the work tip. A couple more niggas got work around here like Fat Man and Derrick but them niggas be in the city hustling a lot; hard to catch them. So, I looked at Bugz to see if I could get a read on his thoughts but that nigga had the same look as always: blank.

"Man, who said that?"

"It don't matter cause their eyes alwayz watching you even when you think they're not."

"Man, Faye said she felted like somebody was watching us the other night."

"Girl got sense then my nigga; just watch what going on around you before you make a move."

"I'll keep that in mind."

"Yeah, you do that."

"Bugz put some fire on this good shit."

"What you got Snoop, some 750 fake out or what?"

I snickered a little bit cause I knew that all this nigga Snoop smokes is that Elvis.

"Is you out yo mind, young nigga? Only the best goes in my lungs."

With that being said, we sat back talking shit for about 30 minutes before Jim-Bob walked back there and said, "Dawg, there's a pack of bad young bitches out front asking for you."

"You don't know who they are, Bob?"

"Nah, my nigga; I can't call it on this one."

That's hard to believe. Bob knows everybody here and in every county around us. But what he said next took me by surprise.

"I think they're from Lexington."

"You sho?"

"Fuck it if they ain't, let's go find out anyway."

I looked at Bugz. This the first time in years I seen this nigga smile; pussy has a way to make even the hardest niggas soft. So we made our way around front. As soon as I got close to the crowd, the girls were standing right in the middle of the dice game. The only person I heard talking was Saint.

"Ya'll need to take ya'll young asses down the street to the kids' party!"

After he said that, one of the older broads stepped straight to the plate to make her point clear.

"Nigga I'm 22 years old ain't nothing a kid can do for me but get they little ass out my face."

"Well, anybody that ain't 18 needs to get to stepping!"

"Negro, please. I brought my little sister down her to see one of ya'll country ass niggas and maybe to see if I could find me one with fat pockets."

"Every nigga in this circle got fat pockets bitch so pick you one!"

"Name calling ain't called for; just trying to see what ya'll bout."

"Like I said, pick one and get the fuck out the way."

Right then I saw Janelle and man she was looking good ass hell.

"Who's looking for me?"

As everybody turned to look my way, Mailman said, "There goes that nigga right there, now move ya'll ass out the middle of the dice game . I'm down."

Once out of the way, my question was answered.

"Me."

"Who is me? Do I know you?"

As I said that, the smile on Janelle's face dropped and she put her head down. I can see big mouth was about to say something stupid so to keep the drama down and from Bugz probably breaking this chick's jaw, I fixed the situation real quick.

"Janelle, I was playing with you."

"Boy, I thought I was going to have to cuss you out dissing me like that front of my sister and all my cousins."

"I know the white girl ain't yo cousin."

"A long story but she's with us so that makes her one of us."

From the dice game, I didn't know which one of them niggas said it, but they told the truth.

"That white girl thick-ass a mutha fucka. I'll take her Dawg if you don't want her fine ass."

With no hesitation, the white girl walked back over to the dice game and started talking to them niggas as did the rest of the girls; seven in all and all of them were nice to eye.

"Janelle, what ya'll doing down here?"

"We heard about the party on the radio right after we left the mall this morning."

"Is that right."

"Look, I'm going to be up front with you. Today's my 18 birthday and school starts next week so what we going to do, stand around all night or have fun?"

Damn. I ain't never had a broad come this strong at me so she caught me off guard but I bounced back real quick.

"It's what ever you want to do."

"You!"

"Look you was straight with me so I'm going to be straight with you. I got a girl."

"And what's that mean? I ain't trying to keep you just fun for one night. Hell I'm going away to the Army after school so I'm getting my fun out the way now."

"Let me get my little cousin home and I'll meet you right here in 20 minutes."

"I ain't going no where; my sister all up on that nigga with the sunglasses on."

"Digg, I'll be back in a few."

"Don't be all night."

"I won't you can bet that."

"Yo Bugz; let's make a move my nigga."

"Why? I'm down $500."

Man that fool lost that money just that fast plus he ain't going with me when I get back might as well let him do his thing.

"Go head; I'll be back in a few."

"All right, my nigga; bark if you need me."

Damn how I'm I going to find this little nigga? I looked at my watch and saw it was a quarter til 1:00 a.m. Maybe he's where I told him to be. I made my way to the corner to see if he's there, but he wasn't. 12:55 a.m. if he's late, Bell is going to act a fool. As I walked back to the park, here L comes running like a run away slave. Sweating like hell and no shirt on.

"Damn L; you cutting it close, baby boy."

"Yeah. Bell said 1:00 a.m. so 1:00 a.m. it is."

"Why you got yo shirt off?"

"I've been dancing all night."

"Cool but look, I need you to get on up the street before you're late."

"Thanks fam for getting me out the house."

"Ain't no thang."

"When you coming home?"

"Don't know baby boy, but get on up the street and click the light on the front porch when you get in."

"Be safe fam."

"Without a doubt, baby boy."

He broke out running up the street. One minute later, the light flashes on the front porch. He's in the house. Now, back to handle some unfinished business named Janelle.

The wee hours of the morning…

Sitting in the Waffle House drinking coffee, the two dumb ass detectives just got through leaving a robbery scene at the Shell Station up on Main Street.

"I'm glad the summer's bout over with. Maybe these robberies will slow down enough for us to catch our breath."

"I know it wasn't none of them boys over on the Northside cause they had the going back to school party and going to school or not everybody goes."

"Shit Chris, they been doing that shit for years."

"Yeah, they have my nephew 'em probably out there having a good time."

"You know they are and some white kids too out there closing the summer out."

"Well Gary I'm a call it a night."

"Me too buddy; it's been a long day."

"I'll be damn. Look who's in that car over at the hotel!"

At the hotel...

Damn. Snoop just told me a couple of hours ago to pay attention to what's go on around me but with a bad bitch all in the car smelling good, I'm all off track. If I had been putting in some work I would've been hit.

"Look, baby girl; you got to get the room."

"Why?"

"I don't turn 18 until next month."

Oooh, I got me a young tender."

"Ain't nothing young bout me."

"Yeah I guess we'll see real soon."

"Yeah we'll see."

"Dawg, who are those two men coming toward the car?"

As soon as my eyes landed on who she's talking about, I slid my .38 under the seat as far as I could get it. I stepped out of the car to short stop them from looking in.

"What's up detectives? Nice night."

"What's up Mr. All State Strong Safety?"

"Not much, just enjoying my last couple of day out before school starts."

As I'm talking to Detective Reeves, Detective Palmer eased his way around my car and was standing right in front of Janelle's window.

"Who's this pretty young thing you got in the car with you?"

"Just a friend, why?"

"It isn't the same girl I seen you with last night."

Damn Faye said she felt like somebody was watching us. And this punk mutha fucka just confirmed it.

"So, what's it to you who I'm with; I ain't doing nothing wrong."

"That's what you say. Hello young lady, may I asks you your name?"

"Janelle."

"That's a real pretty name. Do you know that mister all that got all the girls in town going crazy over him."

"Is that so?"

"I'm afraid so, young lady."

"Well in that case, add me to the list."

All I could do was smile at her answer. This hating ass nigga just tried to put salt in my game I owe him one. By now he's back over on my side looking like he got bitter beer face.

"Chris, leave these kids alone. Besides they're not doing nothing wrong."

"Yeah, if you say so; I'll see you later."

With that, he walked to his car and left but not without looking my way with a real stupid look on his face.

"Look kid, don't worry about him. Are ya'll ready for the season?"

"All I can say is don't miss a game."

"You can bet I won't. When ya'll play Dunbar?"

"Three weeks from Friday."

"Ya'll make us proud."

"We will without a doubt."

"Take care kid and play hard every time you're on the field."

Damn that cracker is really rooting for us.

Up in the room...

Wasn't any talking once we got in the room. Man, ole girl a straight animal. I watch her head bob up and down on my dick, she was looking me right in my eyes; damn that made me weak.

"Ooooh shit, baby."

"You like that, baby?"

"Hell yeah. Do that shit."

She sucked on me until I shot straight down her throat. Damn she didn't miss a drop.

"Let me ride that dick, baby."

"Do you baby girl."

Damn. As she straddled me, she turned around so her ass was facing me and boy was it fat. Slid right down on me and got to bouncing that fat ass like she had hydraulics on it. This pussy was wet as a mutha fucka.

"Damn Nelle, this pussy is wet ass hell!"

"You ain't seen nothing yet, baby."

After a few more minutes of riding me she said, "Baby put it in my ass."

Damn, I ain't never did that before but I sho was about to see what it was like. She stood up, then bent over on all fours. I got at the edge of the bed and she said, "Take your time getting in, baby."

It took a second but damn it was tight and wet. I didn't know I was in her ass at all cause it was so wet. Man, I ran up on a freak bitch and guess what? I loved every second of it.

"Fuck me, baby; yeah, give me that dick!"

Man I lost it when she said that. I couldn't hold off any longer.

"Damn. I'm cumming, baby!"

"Cum in my ass, baby!"

And that I did. Afterwards, we took a shower together and fucked and sucked some more. By the time I busted my 5th nut, the sun was coming up. Damn, what a helluva way to end the summer break.

Chapter 3

The first day of school...

I's been up since 7:00 a.m. bullshitting around the house getting ready plus I ate breakfast with Bell before she left to get her papers and numbers. First period didn't start until 8:35 a.m. and this being my senior year, I don't need but four credits to graduate. I grabbed my book bag and headed for the door.

As soon as I hit the front porch, my nigga from across the street was standing by my 96' Chevy.

"What's up, Zulu?"

"Let me ride with you, fam."

"You know it ain't no thang, my nigga; you my people."

And that's the truth. My granny used to watch him when his mom and dad went to work when he was younger.

"I can't wait until Friday; I'm going to bust one wide open."

See Zulu was a sophomore but he just got home from the boy's camp down in Jackson Kentucky. Nothing but red neck cracker down that way, but the boy show can pack that rock. He was part of the running back by committee, so I don't doubt his statement.

"Ya'll be lucky if I even let the offensive get on the field cause I'm going to try to take every punt I get my hands on to the house."

"I know you ain't lying. Sho hope one of than suckers from Madison Central tackle yo ass."

"They didn't last year, fam."

At the school...

As I pulled up in the student parking lot, it was packed. I'm one of the few black kids that have their own car; the rest of them ride the bus. Guess who's the first person I see? My friend Anthony Lock and he's white. For the past couple of years we'd been real cool; I'd even stayed out to his house a lot. His family is crazy about me. The only difference is, they live out in the country. His dad owns one of the biggest hog farms in the state. Them big, old, nasty hogs eat anything you put in front of them. So when I stayed out there, we'd have to get up and help on the farm, just like everybody else.

"Dawg, what's up bro?"

"Ant you still country ass hell no matter how you try to talk."

"Can't help it just how it is you ready it's going to be a long year?"

"It'll be okay if we win a state title."

"Yes it sure would brother if we could pull that off."

"Damn look at all than girls over there seems like everybodys ass and titty got bigger over the summer."

"Yup look like everybodys been eating beans and corn bread all summer."

"Only yo country ass would say some shit like that but you might be right on this one."

"Lets go in before the home room bell rings."

"Yeah don't want to be late on the first day."

They put us in home room by what your last name starts with so big mouth Cee-Cee was in my home room. Sits right next to me and can you believe it she started in on me early this morning.

"I hope you got your head on straight and leave that hood shit were it belongs!"

"Damn Cee-Cee no hi or good morning just straight to acting like a mother hen."

"Call it what you like but I'm not going to do all your work this year but I'll help you so you'll be ready to take your ACT in two months."

"Thanks Cee-Cee; you know I love you, right."

"Shut up stupid boy!"

All I did was make some kissy faces at her and she'd smile. Let me tell you a little more about Cee-Cee. She is very, very beautiful but here's the catch - she's 6'5. She played on the girls basketball team and they won the girls state title a couple years ago. She had already signed a letter of intent with Purdue University.

"Have you made up your mind were your going to go to school at?"

"Don't start Cee-Cee please you and Bell and Faye plus my momma are nerve wrecking."

"Yeah we love your little ugly ass!"

The lunch period...

Damn, I ain't seen Faye all day so I got me a seat with a couple of the guys off the team. Somebody covered my eyes with their hands. I know it ain't nobody the boys would disapprove of cause you would've never been able to get that close to me. So I waited to see who it was.

"Damn, you smell good whoever you are."

Giggles were all I heard and I was good with sounds. I knew this wasn't Faye. I got a real bad feeling so as soon as I grabbed the hands off my face and saw it was Amanda. Brad, my nose tackle, got a real stupid look on his face. Shit bout to get real ugly. Amanda got her hands all on me and Faye was standing right behind her.

"Excuse me, why do you have your hands all over my man's face?"

Amanda hearing Faye voice must have already had a lie ready cause the bull shit she said had me believing it.

"The cheerleading squad had to pick a senior to represent on the football team to support and Dawg is mine, so I didn't mean nothing by it."

"Oh well, it didn't look right, but in that case, I'm sorry."

"You don't have to say sorry to me, I would've acted the same way if he was mine."

Little did Faye know I'd been freaking with this skinny, big-titty, red headed white girl for about a year off and on. Stone cold freak can't keep her hands to herself when we're alone.

Amanda spoke to all the guys and made her way across the lunch room to where some of her friends were waiting. Once there, they all turned my way and started smiling and waving.

I said to myself I'm going to fuck all them white girls.

"Damn, baby where you been at all morning?"

"I seen you talking to Anthony this morning."

"So why you didn't come over and let me see that sexy smile?"

With that, I knew I had her mind off what just happened.

"Cause I know you hadn't seen him since he got back from his grandparents house."

"I seen him at practice for three straight weeks."

"Ya'll big dummies ain't talked about nothing but football, so save that bull shit for somebody who don't know you."

"Guess you're right; so, what's on your schedule for later?"

"Work and you taking me out to eat afterward."

"That's what's up but I got practice right after school."

"So, I don't get off work until 8:00 p.m. anyway."

"All right, love you I'll see you then."

"Okay, baby; I love you."

Why did I do that front of these big ass dummies. Boy, they had a field day with me.

"Why didn't you tell Amanda you loved her, too?"

That was Brad and Willie giving me the blues. I'm the ladies man of the team but Ant was running a close second.

"Stay out my business and in your playbook some more, Willie so you know what route to run and maybe you'll get same more clock."

"See that's the problem with you boys who play in the secondary. Ya'll all dumb. All you do is roam the field and get all the glory when Brad'em are putting all the pressure on the quarterback to throw a bad pass. How hard is that?"

"Call it what you want but call it first team all district, first team all state and captain of the whole team."

"I can't dispute that one, Dawg."

We all joked a little while longer before we broke back to class. I couldn't help but have the feeling that this year was going to be life changing.

After practice…

Damn practice was rough today with that sun beating down on us. Boy, I couldn't wait to play under the lights Friday night. My watch said 8:30 p.m. and Faye hadn't come out of work yet, so I got out of my car and went in.

Faye looked up and saw me walk in.

"Hi doll, what you still doing working?"

"A few people called in sick so I got to stay until 10:00 p.m. You know I got to go straight home afterward."

"Okay, baby. I'm going home so I'll call you later."

"Okay, baby. Come around here and kiss me, boy!"

Just like sweet candy that kiss got me wanting more than that. Faye could sense it by the way I kissed her.

"Behave, boy; you out of control."

"Sorry baby, you be careful driving them country roads home."

"I will, baby."

"Love you."

"I love you, too."

Over on Teddy Avenue…

As I turned the corner on Teddy Avenue to go home I saw this little black car parked in the lot next to the murder bucket. Ain't no mistaking this car it belonged to Amanda. As I pulled up in the drive way and parked, I knew Bell heard me pull up - she don't miss nothing. I sat in my car for a minute to see if Amanda was going to make a move. Fuck, I might as well go over there and see what's up with her.

"Yo, Dawg; she's been sitting there for about hour."

"Damn, Zulu; where the hell you come from?"

"I've been standing on the side of the house drinking these beers I stole from my old man."

"Damn, nigga, wait until Friday after we bust some ass."

"Fuck that, after the game I got a fifth of Wild Turkey."

"Make sure you save me some."

"Damn, we're going to need two if your thirsty ass is drinking."

"Fuck you, nigga."

"Nah, nigga; fuck that little freak white bitch in that car."

That wild ass nigga walked off laughing; all I could do was shake my head cause that nigga was a soldier all the way.

As I walked over to Amanda's car, I hear the locks pop. I couldn't see in cause her tint was real dark so I got in and closed the door.

"What's up, baby?"

That's all I got out my mouth before she was all over me. I don't know how she done it, but she was naked in a matter of seconds or maybe she was already naked; either way, she was ready.

"Let me suck that dick, baby. It's been a whole month since you let me get some and seeing you today, got my pussy all hot."

After that kiss with Faye, how could I tell her no? I needed relief so she was right on time to help me out with my little problem.

"Handle your business, baby."

She loved it when I talked to her like that. Straight to work, head game on 1000. I laid all the way back in the seat so I could get comfortable while she was doing her thang. I asked myself what make a bitch want to suck on your dick every time they see you. Can't figure that shit out but I ain't mad at her.

"Damn, baby; I'm cumming!"

That made her suck it even harder. Damn that shit was the BOMB.

Chapter 4

Friday, August 29, 1996 – the first game of the year

I woke up this morning with knots in my stomach. I wasn't sick, just couldn't wait to play under the lights. Bell fixed breakfast but wasn't no way I could eat so I hit the door trying to get some air in my lungs. As soon as I got on the porch, I saw Bugz standing by the murder bucket.

"What's up, Dawg? You ready for tonight, my nigga?"

"Ain't no question."

"You know the whole hood going to be up in that bitch."

"Yeah, I know. You and Goldie just make sure ya'll get there."

"Wouldn't miss it for all the tea in China."

"That's what's up, my nigga."

"Oh, by the way, let me get the murder bucket so I can go check on this apartment and shit."

"Bout time nigga; make sure you get a 2 bedroom so I can sit my shit up in that bitch.

"I got you baby boy."

"All right I'll see you after the game."

"Take no prisoners."

"And leave no one alive."

"Sho you right, my nigga."

Damn giving that nigga the bucket would cost us in the long run.

Game time...

Ten minutes until kick off we're about to make our last walk from are locker room to the field. Two-by-two we held hands as we went into battle. Me and Ant were last, bringing up the rear. Our motto was 150 go to war; 150 come home together; no man left behind. On our battle walk, I saw these two young girls. I knew one from my project but the other one, I'd only seen her around school the last couple of days - mainly in the freshmen building. I'd have to check on that later. Right now, the noise was so loud you could barely hear yourself think. You know what that means? High School Football In Kentucky is on!!

Across town, 211 in progress...

As Bugz and Goldie were on their way to the game, something caught Bugz' eye so they pulled into the E-Z Way Mart parking lot. He watched as the woman was closing up the same as Pay Check Exchange. (Yeah, the same one we got a couple of weeks ago).

"I bet that bitch is loaded."

"Fuck it, let's find out."

"I hope this bitch don't make me push her wig back."

As they jumped out the car and started their move, shit was about to get ugly.

"Bitch, drop that bag or I'll drop you!"

Damn, why did that pretty little mixed chick have to hesitate? My man was a wild card all the way.

Two shots rang out.

"Goldie get the bag; I'll be right back!"

Since shit had already gone crazy, Bugz ran up in the E-Z Way Mart and stuck them up, too. It was shift change, so he caught them with the safe open. Bad luck just turned to good. With the old girl on the ground bleeding and the other people locked in the office, they hopped back in the murder bucket and smashed out.

The girl they shot wasn't dead. Matter of fact, she got a good look at the getaway car.

Back at the game...

We were up 28-7 it was going real well. The Fourth quarter had just started and Madison Central about to punt the ball my way. They kicked it away from me all night all I want is one chance at that ball.

"Yo Ant, you and Zulu pitch that wedge tight. If I get a chance, I'm going to bust a move."

They yelled back. "We got you, just hurry up and get through the hole."

With the ball up in the air, my mind went into tunnel vision and all I saw was the end zone. With ball in hand, I made my move and I knew without a doubt, it's 6. On my way to the end zone, all I saw was my whole hood standing in the back of the end zone, the pride I felt was unexplainable having everybody going crazy over what just happen. Damn, that was a helluvalrush just like when I pull my ski mask down. Final score 42 - 10 our way.

Later that night...

The park was fat ass hell; every bodies out. Looking for a reason to have fun and we just gave them one. I was drinking on a fifth of Mad Dog 20;

20 Banana Red. As I hollered at some girls from the hood, I saw someone I wanted to get to know. So I walked over to them.

"What's up LaDonna? Who's your friend?"

"Don't what's up me, nigga. You didn't come over here to talk to me."

"You sho right. Hey baby girl, what's your name?"

"Nicole."

"Nicole? Is that right? Well, Nicole, I'm Dawg."

"I know who you are."

"Do you know how might that be if I just meet you?"

"LaDonna told me who you was."

"She didn't do no hating did she?"

"No but she told me you had a woman."

"And what's that got to do with anything?"

"Cause I don't share so when your free get at me."

With that said she turned and headed over to were her friends were so I just watch on cause I knew somewhere down the line, I would have her.

Just then the murder bucket pulled up and if was full ass a mutha fucka. Damn this nigga is tripping with all than people in my shit. That's my man so I'll play it cool until I can get at him alone. Bugz steps out the bucket and says.

"Catch nigga."

It's another battle of 20/20 that nigga thought he was slick trying to get my mind off what just happened. Plus, I knew those niggas didn't come to the game.

"Nigga, I know ya'll didn't come to the game; what's up with that?"

"Don't trip, my nigga. Something came up, so I had to take care of it."

Only one thing I know of could make this fool miss my game. I bet he done some wild shit, so I'll just wait and see what he got to say.

"Let's walk down the alley."

Half way through, he went in his pocket and pulled out a knot.

"Here's your cut, nigga."

"Tell me you didn't do what I think you did. You know it's hot!"

"Man, shit was right in my face, couldn't let it get away."

"Who was with you?"

"Who you think, nigga? Goldie!"

"That nigga getting high telling that bitch Ken all our business!"

"Man, she's cool Dawg; why you tripping?"

"Nigga fuck cool when we're all sitting down Eddyville (Kentucky State Penitentiary) doing all mutha fucking day!"

"I'll holla at that nigga."

"Yeah, you do that so I won't have too."

"Yeah, I know how that's going to end."

"Well as long as you know, let's have a good time right now."

"Bout time that's what's up."

"Plus how much is this anyway?"

With a little stupid smile on his black ass face he said.

"10,000."

"Damn ya'll come up off that one. "

Police Headquarters – robbery/homicide unit…

"Cris can you believe this shit I was at the fucking game!"

"Well what you want me to do I was with my wife."

"Damn the call came right when that kid was returning a punt."

"Too bad, let's get to work."

Just as Detective Palmer said that his desk phone rang. After a few minutes on the phone and scribbling something down on note pad, he ended the phone call with a smile on his face. "Gray, that young lady just gave a statement to the officer with her."

"What did she have to say?"

"Said she seen what kind of car them two suspect got into."

"That's the best news I've heard in months."

"Well according to you the person whose car she describe was the same person you said was returning a punt at the time of the robbery."

"Telly Shyne!"

"The one and only."

"Well I'll be damn."

"I bet it was Bugz and Goldie. I know it I can feel it."

"Damn that kid's about to throw away a chance of a life time."

"Let's go talk to him first thing in the morning."

"Yeah, let's do that."

The next day...

Bugz must have parked the murder bucket next to my 96' Impala in the wee hours of the morning. He was right on time cause as I go over to wash the 96' and the Robbery/Homicide Detectives were stepping out their car. I know these punk mutha fuckas are on some bull shit.

"Morning, Detectives."

"Nice game last night kid, you look real good returning that punt."

"Thanks."

"You should've had 2 picks but you dropped one."

"Yeah, I know but that's why I play defense and not offense."

"Nevertheless, you played good."

"Thanks. What can I do for you this morning?"

I know what they wanted; I'd seen the news and I couldn't believe that nigga left that bitch alive. One in the shoulder and a graze across the head. With a slip like that and Goldie running his mouth, we're due to catch a bit.

"Well son, someone pointed your car over there out as the getaway car in a robbery."

"How could that be when I was playing in the game last night?"

"Did you let anyone else drive your car?"

"No, that's Bell's car; why would I do that?"

Just then Bell came out the door and walked straight over to where we were talking. "Morning, gentlemen; is there a problem here?"

"No ma'am, Ms. Bell. Just asking a few questions about a robbery last night."

"What's that got to do with my grandson?"

"Well that car was said to be the getaway vehicle."

"What time was the robbery detectives?"

"About 9:15 p.m.

"Well, you know like I do that my baby was on the football field playing for his future."

"Yeah, I know; but did he let anyone else drive that car?"

"I don't play that. He knows that car is in my name so ain't nobody driving that car but him."

"Whose car is this?"

They were pointing at my Chevy.'

"That's my granddaughter's car, why?"

"Who drives this car?"

"Why?"

"Cause I see him driving it all the time."

"Is it a crime for him to drive his sister's car?"

"No, ma'am."

"Any more questions detectives? If not, I would like to get to the grocery store before it gets too crowded?"

"Yes, one more; was that car here last night?"

Without even batting an eye, Bell told a straight lie and put a smile on her face while doing so.

"Yes it was."

"Okay. Thanks for ya'll' time; keep up the good work kid."

"I will, thanks."

As the detectives got in their car and left, I watched Bell cause I knew what next. But it didn't happen until we got back from the store.

"Boy, I ain't going to say this again, keep them two fools out that car."

"Yes, ma'am."

"Don't yes ma'am me, just make sure you do it!"

"I will, Bell."

September 3, 1996...

Damn, it's my birthday. Wonder what I'll get into after school and practice. My cousin L already been in here fucking with me this morning. My momma called and said she'll see me later which is alwayz good. I got dressed and was on my way out the door when Bell came out of her room.

"Happy Birthday, Telly."

"Thanks, Bell."

"Well Bar-B-Q this weekend since it's Labor Day weekend; we'll make a party out of it."

"That's cool, Bell."

"One more thing, grandson. In the white man's world, you're considered a man now, so be careful out there."

"I will Bell, I promise."

"Do me one favor, baby boy?"

"Anything, Bell."

"Put your pistol and ski mask away for a little while."

Before I could say one word, she went back in her room and closed the door. That wouldn't be the last time I hear that today.

At school…

Damn, the day was dragging by real slow. It was fifth period with one more class to go. Art class is cool. I got one of the football coaches. Mr. Travis, or Coach T as we call him, he's all right with me. The bell finally rang on my way to sixth period. I saw Ant and a couple of guys off the team and they had really stupid looks on their faces; I know they're up to something dumb.

I looked for a place to break the crowd in the hallway was thick. As I made my move, someone grabbed my hand and took me in the girl's bathroom. To my surprise, it was Nicole.

"Shhhh!"

Damn, she looked good but where the hell did she come from? In a real low whisper, in the last stall I said, "How did you know I was looking for a way out just now?"

"If you paid more attention to what's going on around you, you would have seen those clowns walking back and forth outside your class."

Damn, does everybody see shit that I don't? I'm slipping; that's bad. Got to check that shit before it gets me in the long run.

"Okay, well thanks for looking out; I'll talk to you later."

"Wait."

"Wait for what?"

"I've got a birthday present for you."

"Oh, you do?"

That's as far as I got cause she had her tongue all down my throat, feeling and touching all on me.

"Whoa, baby girl before you get yourself in some trouble."

"I might like that kind of trouble."

"Yeah, I can dig it, but now ain't the right time. Look where we are."

"Damn, maybe another time; another place."

"Without a doubt it will be."

"Happy Birthday, Telly."

"Thanks, baby girl."

I heard the bell ring so I know I'm late for Coach T's class. As we eased out the bathroom, I'll be damn - guess who's standing right there?

"I know what it looks like Coach T, but it ain't."

"What does it look like then, Telly?"

"Me coming out the girl's bathroom with this young lady."

"Yes, it does."

"I can explain, Coach T."

"I bet you can. Young lady, where are you suppose to be?"

"In biology class."

"I suggest you get there."

"Yes, sir."

On her way down the hall, she turned around and waved. I knew then I would catch her on a later date.

"Boy, leave that young girl alone."

"I didn't do nothing, Coach."

"Yeah, cause you didn't have time."

"Nah Coach T, the guys were up to something dumb so I went in the first door I saw."

"That ain't what they told me."

"They told you I was in the girl's bathroom?"

He smiled and put his hand on my shoulder and we walked to class. When we got there, them dumb asses were right there with a little cake shaped like a football.

"Thanks, guys."

"Don't thank them, thank her."

From the back of the crowd, I saw Faye on her way towards me.

"Thanks, baby girl."

"Your welcome, baby."

I leaned in and stole a kiss as I looked at Coach T, he acted like he was looking at the ceiling.

"Okay, everybody get to where you belong."

"I'll see you later, baby."

"Yes, you will!"

Everybody left but the students who belonged in his class. We ate the cake which I learned later that my mom made it.

"Telly, let me have a word with you."

"Yeah, what's up coach?"

"Have you giving any thought to what you're going to do after school is over?"

"Yeah, Coach; I want to play ball on the next level."

"Well, you better start acting like it then."

"I'm doing my best every time I get on the field."

"The field ain't the problem, it's the off the field stuff that worries me."

"I haven't been in no trouble, Coach T."

"Yeah, but I hear things, Telly."

"Like what?"

"Like I know you and Bugz need to put ya'll Halloween mask and pistols up for a while."

I couldn't say nothing at the moment. I knew the look on my face was a dead give away so I let it ride just like when Bell said it this morning.

"I hear you, Coach."

"Don't hear me boy, make sure you listen to me."

"I got you."

The big game (Dunbar) – late September...

The bus ride to Lexington took all of 20 minutes. We got our ankles wrapped back at home so no time was needed for that. CD player turned up sky-high Master P "Bout it" slamming in my ear. I looked around the bus I was on and I saw nothing but a bunch of small city/country boys ready to go to war. I'll go to battle with these boys any day of the week, 365 days a year. I knew the game was going to be packed cause as our buses brought the football team, cheerleaders and the band had to wait until the police cleared out parking spaces for us to unload. The buzz was loud. The #2 team in the state just made the 14 mile trip into the city to take on the now #3 team in the state after (Louisville St. X lost to #1 Male.) As the game time neared, my stomach was acting a plum fool. Our last trip to the locker room it all came up. Damn was Ant, right there all he says is.

"We're ready now!"

All I did was smile cause I did this before every game. It was something about the lights on Friday. It was game time. On my way to the field, I saw a crowd of niggas standing in the Dunbar home end zone. I'll be seeing that nigga every chance I get.

The game started fast just like we like. We were up 10-3 going in the second quarter with Dunbar punting the ball to us. Me and Zulu lined up in a double punt return. The ball was in the air. I go deaf; all I could hear was my heart beating and the wind blowing a little to the left. The time was now. With the ball in my hands, I faked the reverse to Zulu and took it back as I turned the corner. I picked up a couple of blocks on the way no one left but the punter; man, ain't no way I'm going to let this punk tackle me. As I got close to him, I knew he heard me when I said, "You're a bitch!"

I made a hard cut to the left and left him hugging the air touchdown. But as soon as I saw dude, he had his hand out, so I trotted around the back of the end zone and handed him the ball.

"That's $500 and I'll be seeing you again real soon."

"That was luck, country nigga!"

"We'll see, city boy."

Dunbar was back on offense, but not for long. Ant called out the defensive play, "Double stunt, stack cover, 2 man under!"

See, that's why I got love for this white boy this play let me hide so the quarterback thinks I'm helping with the run and was he oh so wrong. As soon as he threw the ball, his eyes let me know he made a boo-boo. That ball was mine, back to the house I go.

"I told you I'd be seeing you real soon."

"You still some shit!"

"Some shit with an extra stack and counting; I ain't done yet."

After the extra point and the kick off, the half time horn sounded. 24-3 our way. At the half, Coach Mack talked to us about not letting up. On our way out, Coach T pulled me to the side and asked me why I kept talking to the same guy in the end zone. I wouldn't lie to him so I told him.

"I met that dude at the mall a couple of weeks ago and he said he'd give me $500 every time I brought him the ball, plus he said Dunbar was going to kick our ass and called us country."

The country part I knew would get under Coach T's skin cause he was really from a small town in northern Kentucky called Carrollton.

"Well you better keep taking him the ball then."

"Every chance I get."

"You do that, baby boy."

And do that I did but just one more time for a total of 3 touchdowns, so that $1500 the final more 45-13 we roll again. After a news interview with 18 Action News, I made my way over to the buses. On my way, I ran into the dude, Von.

"You did good, country nigga; here's your money."

"Nah, I can't take it. That's what I do on Friday nights."

"Nah, young nigga; you earned it so it's yours."

"Thanks, fam."

"I'll be seeing you again."

Damn. I get on the bus Zulu, Ant, Willie, and a couple of guys I really click with were waiting on me so I put my head phones on and handed everybody some of the money. I just made off dude I know they want to party a little and those hundred dollar bills will come in handy. I took my headphones off and said, "Wounds will heal, blood will fade, but pride is forever."

Tyrene "Topp Dawg" Collins

Chapter 5

October, 1996 – early Saturday morning...

Damn we're undefeated and things were going real good. I was on my way to take the ACT with Cee-Cee. Boy, she's really been on my ass and so has Bugz; that nigga is broke again.

"Cee-Cee, turn that shit down."

"Nah, nigga. You should've took yo ass home last night after the game!"

"You know I couldn't do that."

"I don't see why not. Your future is at stake and you bull shitting."

Man how could I do that after we beat the shit out of Franklin County last night.

"I hear you, doll."

"Don't hear me, nigga; listen some damn time!"

"I love you, too."

"Shut up, ugly boy."

Bugz' new apartment...

Like a true stick up kid, my man Bugz was up early this morning thinking about a come up. I knew he would blow his money on dumb shit and now he was ready to go back to work. So, he picked up his phone and called Goldie.

After a few rings, Goldie answered, "Yeah?"

"You woke nigga?"

"Yeah, been up for a minute."

"What yo pockets look like?"

"They short ass a mutha fucka.'

"Well, let's see what's popping this morning."

"Man, you know Dawg said it's hot since we pulled that last move."

"Man, that nigga was gone to take the ACT so quit crying like a little girl and let's make a move."

"You know that nigga has been on my ass lately."

"We'll just make his cut a little bigger, that's all he cares about anyway."

"True. Let me drop Ken off and I'll be through."

"Hurry up, nigga; you know shit is real sweet early in the morning."

"I hear you, my nigga."

"Nah, feel me cause I'm hungry as the Werewolf of London."

Test time…

Once we got to the testing place, I tried to shake Cee-Cee but she was sweating me like a cheap suit. I knew there were going to be same bad bitches up in here. And what do you know, I was right. One stood out cause I knew her and she was looking real good. I eased up next to her as I whisper, "Damn, Janelle; you look real good early this morning!"

Without turning around or even looking my way, she gave me goose bumps.

"Mr. all that and then some, how you been doing?"

"I can't complain; just living and doing my thang."

"Yeah, I know. I see you on T.V. every Friday night doing you thang."

"I try, baby girl. But what's up? I thought you were going to the Army after school?"

"Well my mom got sick and I didn't want to be too far from her."

"Sorry to hear that."

"That's okay. Who's that tall bitch looking all crazy?"

"That's my people; don't worry about her."

"Well, you can tell her to get out my mouth."

"Nah, I'll leave that to you."

What she did next, turned me red cause she caught me off guard. She leaned right over and kissed me right on my lips. I know Cee-Cee was going to tell Faye. Damn; her lips were soft.

"Good luck on your test."

"Yeah. You, too."

With that said she got up and went over to where some other girls were sitting watching us the whole time with smiles all over their faces.

I had to find me a seat in the back cause Cee-Cee had steam coming out of her ears.

Hitting a major lick…

After Goldie picked up Bugz, they rode across town to the Hillside looking for a come up. And luck was on their side. They pulled up to the Kroger's and were about to hit The National City Bank at the front of the store. Just as they pulled up, one of Kroger's night managers came sliding out the side door carrying two nice size money bags - BINGO.

"Nigga, look at that fool looking around all crazy."

"If he knew what was about to happen, he would shit in his pants."

"Yeah, my nigga, but don't bust yo banger if you don't have to. We don't need the heat while we're trying to get away from this bitch."

"Nigga, what da fuck you talking about if that nigga even hesitates, I'm going to push his wig back; won't be no living witnesses this time, bet dat."

"True, my nigga; dis on the North!"

"Money in site means money bout to be right."

On my way home…

Cee-Cee didn't said one word to me. I knew she was hot about that little episode with Janelle, but what was I to do. So I do my best to break the ice.

"You hungry, Cee?"

"Nigga, please; you got some nerve!"

"What you talking about?"

You know how black women are when you insult their intelligence, popping and rolling her neck all "Who's that bitch all up in your ugly face!"

"Some girl I just met, why?"

"Be for real, Telly; that ho kissed you on your nasty lips!"

"Can't help if she wanted something sweet in her life early this morning."

Saying that dumb shit put a little smile on Cee-Cee's face so I knew I had her, so I laid it on a little thick.

"Let's go to the food court in the Fayette Mall and get something to eat; plus, I'm a buy you something to wear for homecoming."

"Nigga, you think you slick trying to buy me? That's cool, but your wrong for fucking over Faye. You know that girl loves you."

"Don't tell her you saw that bullshit."

"I don't want to hurt her cause your dumb ass don't know how to act."

"Thanks, Cee."

"Don't thank me; hope you got a bank roll on you!"

"Whatevea you want, I got you."

"Yeah, we're going to see."

"I guess we will."

211 in progress…

Bugz and Goldie slipped out of the car. On their way over, another employee came out the door and I be damn if he didn't see them coming, but it was too late. Bugz, being the closest one to him, put his finger up to his lips and pointed his gun at the guy's head, he made the move on the money while Goldie held that guy at bay.

"All I want is the money so don't be no hero."

The guy goes to say something but Bugz swung his Mossburg Riot Pump shotgun like a baseball bat and broke dude jaw.

"I told your stupid ass don't be no hero look what you made me do!"

"AAAhhhhhhh."

That was all the guy could do with his jaw shatter. Bugz picked up the two money bags and they felt heavy.

"What we going to do with him?"

"Put his punk ass in the trunk of that car; better yet, put both of them in this mutha fucka!"

They made both guys get in the trunk and made their way back across the parking lot like nothing happened. On their way back to Bugz's spot, a serious conversation started.

"Bugz, those bags looked real heavy, my nigga."

"Yeah may just be the change and shit but I know we'll get a few thousand."

"That's straight but what we going to tell Dawg?"

"That nigga ain't going to trip cause all he cared about was getting some money."

"Yeah I know, but that shit got our name wrote all over it."

"Why you crying like a bitch?"

"That nigga been on some bullshit with me lately so I just don't want no shit behind this."

"Quit getting high with them bitches and telling our business and there won't be no problem."

"Man, I ain't getting high."

"Save that shit for a nigga who don't know you."

"Man, fuck ya'll; I'm grown!"

"Say that shit to Dawg."

"What's he going to do if I do?"

"Well, you know like I know that he fucks with that rich white kid from the county so don't come up missing and shit cause you know them hogs eat anything you put in front of them."

Why did he have to go off and say all that about Ant and the hogs. That wasn't for everybody to know cause in the future little did he know those hogs would save us more then once.

"Man, lets just count the money so I can go buy some work."

"What you talking about some work?"

"I'm going to holla at Pooh and get a couple of zone."

"Man, that nigga be up in Lexington out in Winburn on Ward Drive. How you going to find that nigga?"

"Easy, he's family; I got his number."

"Dawg, did say something about hollering at Fat Man or Derrick."

"Ya'll need to and let the stick up shit cool off."

"I'm a look into that."

"Let me know I'll call that nigga and tell him we're on our way up."

"Nah, got to see what Dawg wants to do."

"Since you said it probably a lot of change, give me a couple of grand so I can roll."

"You sure you don't want to count it with me?"

"Nah, $2900 will get me four and a half so I'll drop you at your spot so I can make my move."

"Fuck it. If you say so, I got $3000 at my spot. I'll run upstairs and give you that."

"Yeah, that's cool."

"If you say so."

Little did he know he missed out on a lick of a lifetime. Trying to hurry up and catch Pooh so he could buy some work had him all off track. You know what they say slipper count in this GAME...

Later that night...

On my way to Bugz spot, I stopped by Dre's and got some beers and a couple of half pints. Since I ain't 21, I go to the boot legger; they all know me cause my old man was loved around town. The hood called him Ging, but to me, he was plain ol' dad. He died a couple of years ago in a car wreck. I saw some of his old partners, so I kicked it with them for a second.

"Tiger, what's up old man?"

"Boy, if I had yo hands, I'd throw mine in the Kentucky River."

"My hand ain't all that good."

"Baby boy, you got the best hand right now, just don't fold it too soon."

"I won't. What you drinking on? It's on me."

"Just a little E&J and coke."

"Get two, I'm about to bounce on up out of here."

"Thanks, baby brother; you take care out there."

"Tell Gunnz and Bo-Dean I said what's up?"

"Okay, be safe."

Once I got to Bugz house I saw some cars in the parking lot that looked familiar but I didn't pay it no mind. I knocked on the door and my nigga throws the door wide open.

"What took you so long getting over here?"

"I stopped through the Bottoms and got a couple of drinks."

"What for? I got Gunnz to ride with me to the liquor store and got all we need."

"Nigga, I ain't know!"

"Whatevea, my nigga; just get in here."

"Damn, you really sitting it out?"

He had liquor and weed everywhere plus a bunch of leaching ass niggas all up in his spot.

"Man let me holla at you in the back."

"Ole girl in my room, so go in yours; I'll be back there in a second."

On my way I spoke to all the homies up in there and some of the girls from the hood I knew then that this spot wouldn't last long.

In the room, I sat up as my own. I got a chair, a mattress on the floor and that's it. I sat in my chair and waited 5 minutes before Bugz came in the room.

"Damn, my nigga; you show spending yo money real reckless."

"That shit ain't nothing, but peep this, remember how you was talking about getting in the dope game? Well, let's see what it do."

"I'm cool. I got enough money to probably get a real nice package for us."

"Fuck probably, my nigga."

As he said that, he threw me a brown sack wrapped up and this bitch was heavy.

"Tell me you didn't do what I think you done."

"Man, it was right in my face; I couldn't let it get away!"

I know this nigga, he's lying; but that's my nigga, so I let it ride.

"Who was with you?"

"Me and Goldie, why?"

"Man, what I tell ya'll? You know we hot from that last shooting and you left that bitch alive."

"Ain't nothing, Goldie was in such a big rush to get at Pooh about some work, he don't know how much money he left behind."

"What you talking about?"

"I gave him the $3000 I had left and he smashed out without helping me count the money."

"That nigga is tripping real bad; he needs to leave that shit alone."

"He's grown. Why don't you stay off that niggas ass?"

"Man, I ain't on his ass. I just want that nigga to be straight when we blow up."

"That nigga would die and go to hell for you."

"I know. How much money in this sack?"

All I got was a big-ass smile. So I opened it myself and looked in. Upon looking in, I jumped up and locked the door.

"What the fuck did you do?"

"Caught the night manger coming out of Kroger's."

"Did you have to kill anybody?"

"Nah, but I hit that fool in the jaw with my shotgun like Sammy Sosa hitting a homerun."

I knew that if he did what he said, that mutha fucka's jaw was going to be wired shut for months.

"How much?"

$82,000 a piece, not counting the change."

"Let's get right to it so niggas will think we're hustling."

"It's on you, Dawg. You call the shots; I'm with you either way."

"Give me $50,000 and I'll put $50,000 with it and in a couple of days, we'll see what it do."

"Ain't no thang, baby boy; now, let's go party!"

"Nigga, hell nah. I'm going home with my money and the $50,000 you gave me, so go get it."

"Why you leaving?"

"Cause you got to many niggas and bitches in our business."

"I'll put they asses out, if you want me to."

"Nah, my nigga; enjoy yourself cause we're about to get our hustle on."

"That's what's up, my nigga."

"By the way, we're putting our masks and guns up for awhile."

"Tru?"

"Now go get that money, so I can get up out of here."

"Say no more."

Chapter 6

Homecoming

Talking about bubble guts, when I got up this morning my stomach was in knots. Bell tried to make me eat but it was too early. So I told her I would eat something at lunch time. And very little was going down then.

I tell you why all state runback Shawn Alexander and Boone County was coming to town. (Yeah the same one who set the SEC freshman rushing record for the most yards in one game and The NFL MVP in 2005.) So, now you see why I'm all tight.

While I'M sitting on the trainer's table getting my ankles tapped, Ant walked in but didn't say one word. Nothing needed to be said. Now game time is upon us and the Lord's Prayer was heard throughout the whole locker room. On the battle walk, hand-and-hand with Ant, I saw Faye and Cee-Cee and boy they looked real good. Cee-Cee smiled. Faye blew kisses. Damn, no time for that shit right now. The closer we got to the field, the brighter the lights. What could I say - this is what I live for!

Robbery/homicide unit...

The two numb nut detectives were trying to figure out what was going on with all the robberies around town. Well, really Palmer cause Reeves was trying to get to the game.

"Gary, why don't you go to the game cause you're just in my way?"

"Are you sure?"

"Yeah, now leave before I change my mind."

"Why don't you come with me? That kid Alexander is the best in the state."

"We'll see tonight with the number one defense in the state."

"Hope those boys stand up tonight."

"They will; you know those boys are the pride of the town."

"You know that's right, I'll see you later."

"Maybe we'll get lucky on one of these cases real soon."

"Don't worry, partner; we'll get a break."

"Hope you're right."

"I'm alwayz right."

"Yes, you are."

Game time...

Man this country-ass nigga ran the ball hard as hell. He broke one and I had to tackle his country ass. When I hit him he got up and said, "I'll be seeing you a lot tonight."

"I'll be here waiting on you, too."

With a smile on his face he jogged back to the huddle and was he right - that nigga was down field the whole first half.

Halftime score was 17-7; their way. We ain't never trailed at the half. The locker room was real quiet. Faces had a look I'd never seen before. I was real tight; couldn't shake this feeling.

Coach talked during the half, but I don't think anyone in that locker room heard one word he said.

On our way out, Ant got next to me and whispered, "Dawg, I don't want to lose my last homecoming."

"We won't."

The second half started and the offense put seven on the board immediately (17-14); Boone County by three. After that, both defenses stood strong. The fourth quarter rolled around and with sixteen seconds left on the clock, Boone County punted the ball to us. This was our last chance to keep a perfect record.

In the huddle, my only request was, "Ya'll pick' em up and I'll take care of the rest."

Me and Zulu lined up again in the double punt formation. I knew they were going to kick it away from me, but me and Zulu got a trick up our sleeves.

Ball in the air, no noise could be heard. Just as I thought, they kicked the ball away from me. I acted like I was going to block, but I broke back around Zulu and he tossed me the ball.

They never saw it coming I'd never had it this easy returning a punt. As I reached the end zone, I heard the final buzzer sound. I didn't even look back. I kept running straight to the locker room. I wanted to tell the Lord thanks personally.

The dance and after party…

The feeling is unexplainable. I kept our team from our first loss of the season. Fresh out of the shower, getting ready for the dance, dressed from the waist down - all Polo, my man Ant came over.

"Dawg, that was awesome what you did."

"Couldn't have done it without ya'll."

"Yeah, well thanks. You made this night one to remember, bro."

"Don't think me, we're a team."

"If you say so, but you got some people who want you at the locker room door."

Hoping it was the news, I didn't put on my shirt trying to show off and that I did, but it wasn't the news. It was Amanda and half the cheerleading squad. They got their eyes full and had a little smile on their faces that let me know I could fuck them all.

"Amanda, what you doing here?"

"Just wanted to let you know I got you something to drink in my car."

"Yeah, that's cool but I got to get up with Faye in a few so I won't be able to see you tonight."

"I know, just came by my car and get the stuff is all I ask."

"Okay, I'll be there in a minute."

"I'll be waiting."

I knew this was going to be a wild night and one to remember. I went back in the locker room and finished getting dressed so I could go to the dance.

On my way out with a Gatorade in my hand, Ant says, "Don't do nothing I wouldn't do, bro."

"So that means do everything."

"You got that right, bro."

As I walked to the parking lot to go to Amanda's car, I poured out the Gatorade so I can put my drink in the bottle. Damned near there, mind on getting fucked up, I see Bugz and a couple more nigga from around our way.

"What's up, star? Where you going?"

"To get this drink from Amanda."

"You still fucking with that white bitch?"

"Not really; just having fun."

"Yeah right, but dig what time you coming to the hood?"

"After the dance, why?"

"Cause nigga, we wanted to kick it with you."

"Tru, I'll be there right after the dance."

"Have fun, my nigga; I'll see later."

Back to my mission, getting to Amanda's car. Two cars away, I saw her standing by her car. It was a little dark where her car was at so I knew she was up to something. Before I could even say a word, she had her tongue down my throat.

"Hold up, baby. Damn, where's my drink at so I can put it in this bottle so I can take it in the dance?"

"On the back seat. I got you a bottle of Segram's gin and a banana red Mad dog."

"Damn, you trying to get me fucked up for real."

"And to congratulate you on a great game."

I know what's on her mind and before I could stop her, she had me pushed up on the car and was working on my belt. Fuck it; I let her handle her business. Dick all in her mouth, my head rolled back; I didn't hear Willie walk up on us.

"Damn, Dawg; that shit looks like it feels good!"

"Man, it feels good as a mutha fucka."

Amanda looks up and saw Willie and her friend Tiffany all under his arm then went right back to what she was doing. For those people who don't know, white girls are super freaks.

"Man, enjoy yourself; I'll see you inside."

"I can't with you fucking with me."

They walked off laughing. By now, I knew I had to hit that pussy so I said. "Pull that dress up and panties to the side."

"About time you gave me sum of the chocolate dick!"

"Bend over and grab yo ankles, baby."

She did as she was told; that pussy was soaking wet and I slid right in.

"Ooooh baby, that dick feels good."

"You going to let me cum in yo mouth?"

"You can cum where ever you want to baby."

A few minutes more and I pulled out and cummed all in her mouth. I be damn if she ain't smiling like she just won the lottery. That's why I keep fucking with this freaky-ass white bitch.

The party goes on...

I went back to the locker room to clean up so I wouldn't smell like her cause I knew Faye would be going to be all up on a nigga. After I get together I headed to the dance, bottle in hand, I heard the music jumping "The Atomic Dog" was playing and I knew my people were being ass nasty as they wanted to be.

As I went through the doors, I saw all the girls bent all over with my niggas standing right behind them grinding like a mutha fuckas.

The teachers were trying to separate them but as soon as they did, they're right back at it. That puts a smile on my face cause we acted the same way every time that song comes on - NASTY.

Halfway across the room, Mrs. Carmen stoped me and ask, "Telly what's in the bottle?"

"Just Gatorade. You know we played hard tonight so I need my fluid to put back in me."

"Yes, you did. You boys make me proud."

"Thanks, we do our best."

"Go enjoy yourself and try not to act like these other bad children."

"I'll try but can't make no promises."

With that I kept it moving but that was short stopped cause just like I said, Faye would be all up on me and there goes my baby.

"Damn, bout time you got here."

"Had to make sure I was fresh for you."

"And you do look fresh and smell real good."

"You want some of this drink?"

"Boy, get that stuff out my face; you know better."

"Tru, let's go dance, this is my shit!"

Jodeci was on. They were playing "*Forever My Lady*" and you should have seen everybody all hugged up; I mean everybody. I held Faye so tight I could feel her heart beat. Something in me knew this wouldn't last forever cause she hadn't done nothing or been nowhere, so I knew life would separate us soon. It would hurt at first, but the way I was living, it was just a matter of time. But fuck it right now; I'm a play it how it goes.

"Faye, let's bounce. I want to go to the hood; they're waiting on me."

"Okay, let me tell Cee-Cee."

"Did you drive, baby girl?"

"Nah, Cee-Cee came and got me."

"Good, cause this drink got me feeling real good."

"That's cool but I'm gonna make you feel better than that later."

"I know that's right."

Chapter 7

No turning back now...

Last night was off the hook. Me and Faye stayed at the hotel and got our freak on and boy it was real good. But now I'm bout to go holla at Snoop to see what's up with the work. I knew this nigga was up this morning so I knock real light on the door.

"Who is it?"

"Dawg."

He opened the door with gun in hand and blunt hanging from his lips, he gave me same pounds and closed the door behind me.

"What's up, my nigga?"

"Quiet down, young nigga. Ta-Ta back there asleep."

"My bad, but peep this, I'm trying to get some work."

"I got a little; what you want."

"Bout a $100,000 worth."

The look on his face said he didn't believe me so I showed him the loot.

"Damn nigga, you trying to get deep in the game quick."

"I want to get paid in a major way."

"Let me make a phone call and see if my man is awake."

"What do you want me to do?"

"Sit still and be ready to ride to the city."

Twenty minutes later, fully dressed, Snoop came back out front and asked, "You strapped, young nigga?"

I looked at that nigga like he was crazy cause with all this money on me, I wasn't bout to let no nigga come up off me.

"Don't move without it."

"Tru. We're going to meet my man, Shorty."

I knew a little about Shorty. Him and his partner Dirty come down here to shoot dice but word on the streets was Shorty killed some niggas down south to get on. Either way, I knew I was going for broke.

On the ride to the city, I watched what way we were going and just like I thought, we headed for East Inn. So I asked Snoop, "What am I going to get for my money?"

"Four and half is the best I could get you."

"As long as I double my money."

"Do it right and you'll do more then double."

"That's what I'm talking about."

Rest of the ride I was quiet, counting dollars in my head and boy did I count a lot. We pulled up in the back of the projects (Arbor Groove) and a few wild-looking niggas were out getting early morning money.

"Be still; I'll be right back."

With my money in his hand, Snoop jumped out of the car and I heard a couple of them niggas call him, "Georgetown."

Now I know these niggas had seen him before. I relaxed just a little bit but yet with a watchful eye. Bout twenty minutes later, Snoop came back out and hopped back in the car and threw a bag on the backseat. I didn't say nothing at first, but it was getting the best of me.

"What's it look like?"

"Shit all there and he sent you a sack of that good shit, but you don't need it so I'll keep it for you."

"I don't care, is the work good?"

"When we get back home, I'll show you and from there, you're own your own."

"That's all I need."

Paper chase...

I ain't never seen that much work. He showed me how to rock it up but I wasn't paying any attention cause I knew I would go over to Leach's house. That's an old nigga from our hood who lives up on West Street.

"Dawg, you see how I did that?"

I lied just so I could get up out of there, "Yeah, but that shit looks hard."

"Just don't pour none of this shit down the drain when it looks like water."

"I hear you, my nigga."

"Okay, be safe out there; shit is for real."

"Tru, thanks for the hook up. What I owe you?"

"Just don't mention my name if shit goes bad for you."

"I know the rules."

"Dawg, one more thang, my nigga."

"What's that?"

"Take this Mac 11 with you and stand on any nigga in your way."

"Man this some New Jack City shit good looking."

School and hustling...

Man, two games left and then the playoffs. I couldn't stay focused on school. Kept thinking about getting money. I knew Bugz could handle why I'm doing this, but my mind is there with him. Still undefeated, we played Tates Creek Friday and then it's senior night Louisville (Seneca) is coming to town.

On my way to Chemistry class I saw Ant, "Dawg, you seem somewhere else, you okay?"

"Yeah just a few things on my mind, that's all."

"Why don't you came stay in the country for awhile? Mom and dad been asking when your coming down."

"You know what? That sounds like a good idea."

"I'm going home after practice and get some clothes then I'll call you to come get me."

"All right, bro; that's a bet."

Little did I know, me going to the country for a couple of days would cost me dearly; but fuck it, I need a break.

Bugz spot...

My man was counting the money and Goldie was sitting by watching. It was short and he couldn't figure it out. All the work was almost gone and the profit wasn't what he thought it should be. The re-up was even short ten stacks. With the wheels rolling in his head, shit is about to get ugly.

"Damn, I don't want to hear this niggas mouth!"

"What the fuck you been doing with all that work?"

"What the fuck you mean what I been doing with the work?

"Ya'll had plenty, so what you do with it?"

"I've been breaking it down, putting it on the streets."

"Well, I guess you've been fucking it up cause ain't no way you should be short."

"Look at this shit I got left and tell me what you think shit's bagged up in quarter and halves."

Bugz went to the back and brought back what was left of the work and boy did he really fuck up.

"Here nigga, put this half on the eyes."

Goldie drops the half on the scales and what he sees let him know Bugz is a tru stick up man and not a dope boy.

"You've been giving away this much to everybody who buys a half?"

"Yeah, why?"

"Dumb ass nigga, you giving them too much."

"How's that? Twenty grams is a half."

"Man, Dawg didn't show you shit. Nigga, a half is 14 soft, 12 hard; you done give away damn near a brick and a half."

"Get the fuck out of here. Who told you that, nigga?"

"Man, I've been hustling on the side. Ya'll don't alwayz take me with ya'll."

"Fuck it, I'll make it up the best way I know how."

"Dawg said be easy with the pistol play."

"Shut up, nigga, He's gone to country for a while with that white boy, Ant!"

"Why he alwayz going out there?"

"Fool, them white folks love that nigga."

"Well, I'm with you, my nigga."

"Yeah, I bet you are."

Why the country is so beautiful...

I went home and told Bell I was going out to the country for a couple of days she just smiled cause she knew I wouldn't be in no bull shit. Told her I'd be back home Sunday night. On the way out the door I told her, "Look for me on the news Friday night; I'm a blow you a kiss."

"I'll be looking for my kiss."

Ant was sitting outside talking to Zulu so I knew he was straight, that's why I wasn't in no rush to get out the door.

"You ready, bro?"

"Yeah, let's roll so I can ride the 4 wheeler before it gets too dark."

"Not today, we got some work to do."

"Man, I ain't fucking with them stinking ass hogs tonight."

Ant smiled so now I knew some bull shit was going on.

"That's between you and dad."

"Well, I guess I'll see what Big Ant wants done. See you at school, Zulu."

"Yeah, fam; don't let one of them big, ole mean hogs bite you in your ass."

With that, he walked off laughing.

It was a nice ride way down to Burton Pike so I closed my eyes and took in the smell of the country.

Thursday, the day before kickoff...

I'd been in the country for a couple of days and things were looking better. I hadn't worried about hustling or the streets. Me and Ant pulled up at school and I be damn if Amanda and her friends weren't standing there. I knew shit was about to get real interesting.

"Ant, you see the look on Amanda's face?"

"Yeah, bro; she's got it bad for you."

"I know but I got to let her go; she's going to Northern Kentucky University next year."

"Man, just have fun. You're going somewhere next year too, so don't worry."

"I guess you're right."

Before I could even get out of Ant's truck, all the girls were right at my window. I looked at Ant and all he did was smile as he rolled my window down.

"Hello, ladies."

All of them smiled but Amanda spoke right up. "Hi, Dawg and Ant. What ya'll doing together so early this morning?"

"He's been staying out to my house for the last couple of days."

"You mean to tell me you've been staying in the country and I didn't know it?"

"Just trying to stay focused so we can close out the season the right way."

"Don't you worry about being focused; I'll be to see you tonight."

Before I could protest, she and her friends walked off. I looked at Ant and said, "Why did you tell her that?"

"Man, you need some pussy and maybe that will help you tomorrow so quit crying and let's go before the bell rings."

Getting the money right before Dawg comes home...

Every since Bugz found out he was the one who fucked up the money, he'd been a time bomb waiting to blow, drinking heavily and trying to figure out a way to make it right before I get home.

"Wake up, Kay. I've got to take you home; I got shit to do."

"I'm going stay here until you get back."

"What the fuck I just say? Now so get yo ass up before I help you up!"

Kay looked at that nigga and she seen death in his eyes for somebody and she knew it wasn't go to be her.

"Okay, give me a minute and I'll be ready."

"You got that but let me come back in here and you ain't ready, shit ain't going to go like you think."

As Bugz leaves the room Kay rushes to get dressed and now she knows she's fucking with a full fledged nut case. After dropping her off, the mission was set. The first spot he saw that looked like it was sweet was going to get an F-4 tornado through their front door. He jumped on 460 East going toward Paris but something caught his eye. He turned left behind the Long John Silvers - a Farmer Bank was sitting right there.

He parked in the Long John's parking lot and watched for a second to see what was moving and boy what he saw was a came up - some old, white man with a money bag was walking to the bank from his truck. Down comes the mask, pistol in hand, it was now or never.

Some fool saw him coming and screamed at the old man. When the old man turned and seen what was happening, he went for his gun.(That's right, in Kentucky everybody packs a gun) The move was a bust but the person who gave the old man the warning would never be able to tell no one else nothing. Bugz turned on his heels and made his way over there with one thing on his mind - kill. And kill is what he did. Two shots rang out; wouldn't be no witnesses to tell which car he got in cause the second shot blew her brains smooth out. The heat we would feel for this would be on our asses for years.

He got back in the car, getting ready to jump on the highway like nothing ever happen.

Ant's house when the stars are out...

Me and Ant were standing on the side deck of the house chilling when Big Ant came out; I knew he was about to get serious. "Hi boys, it's a nice night out."

We just nodded our heads and waited and listened to what was coming next; damn shit was coming.

"Telly, you know I hear things being that a lot of people I do business with are in high places, so what I'm about to say is for you and you only. If you don't stop that foolishness you're doing, you're going to end up dead or in prison for a long time. That's the only time I will say that so what ya'll going to do tomorrow night?"

Before we could answer the last question, some headlights turned in the driveway I knew who's car that was.

Big Ant looked at us and smiled. Standing up to leave he said "You boys behave and don't be out here all night; school is in the morning and the game is tomorrow night."

By the time Amanda and Tiffany got out of the car, we met them halfway down the driveway. Ant didn't say shit, he just wrapped his arms around Tiffany and headed to the guess house. I looked at Amanda and she looked good standing there in her skin-tight, Scott County sweatsuit and flip flops even though was a little cool out.

"What ya'll doing out here?"

"What you thought? You were going to stay out here and not see me."

"Nah, it ain't that; it's just we got a game tomorrow."

"Well, we ain't got all night, so let's go!"

"Okay, baby, but just once."

"Yeah, right; it takes at least three times before I get warmed up."

I knew then I was in for a long night and shit would tell on me later.

"Just be easy I tried from practice."

"Don't worry, baby; I got you."

By the time we got to the guest house, Ant was laid back getting his dick sucked so I knew he was behind this little get together.

"Ant, you ain't shit."

"Yeah, but you'll thank me later."

I didn't get another word out cause Amanda had me down on the couch with my sweat pants down around my ankles and my dick in her mouth. I still ain't figured it out; white girls don't have no problem freaking in front of each other and boy did they put on a show to the wee hours of the morning. Last thing I remember was busting in Amanda's mouth before I fell out. Damn.

Chapter 8

Together we stand, nothing but pride on the line…

Friday morning and boy had me and Ant really fucked up. All night freak session so the day was pure hell. Every class I'd been asleep. Got in trouble in chemistry class; damn near got sat out of tonight's game. So art class rolled around and Coach T watched me drag in, all he did was point toward the door and said, "Take your sorry butt to the locker room and lay down."

"I'm fine, Coach T."

"I heard from all your teachers that you've been asleep in their class room. And, not just you; Anthony, too."

"But."

"Don't but me; I don't know what ya'll called ya'll self doing, but you better not let us down tonight."

Before I could answer, he walked back over to the rest of the class. So I turned on my heels and made a straight line for the locker room. When I got there, Ant was already laid out on one of the couches half asleep looking real stupid.

"Man, I told you shit would catch up with us."

"Yeah, yeah, but it was fun, wasn't it?"

"You ain't never lied; that little freak ate me alive."

"I don't know what you were doing to that girl, but I bet mom and dad could hear her screaming like a wild woman."

"That bitch be over reacting; she can take a whole leg up in that pussy."

We both laughed and I went over to the big lazy boy and stretched out. It was sixth period so I knew half the team would be making their way down here. So I tried to get a little rest but it was too late. Them fools started rolling in, hyped up out their fucking minds.

Robbery/homicide unit Friday afternoon

Detective Palmer's hair was falling out cause of yesterday's homicide. The old man gave them an account of the events that happened. Hard to believe that woman lost her life behind a robbery gone bad.

"Gray, what are you over there doing?"

"Listening to the local news talk about yesterday."

"Ain't nothing we don't already know so get over here and help with this paper work."

"No can do partner; got me a half day I'm going home and lay down then I'm going to the game."

"You're an asshole, you know that don't this shit bother you?"

"Yeah but your problem is you think too hard. See, the way I see it they'll slip up and fall right in our hands."

"I guess you're right; hope they slip up soon."

"Don't worry, at the rate they're going, they will so you be easy. I'm gone."

"Be careful and enjoy the game."

"Enjoy! Will be easy; we're playing Tates Creek."

"Don't underestimate those boys; anything can happen."

"We're not anything; we're the #2 team in the whole state so ROLL BIG RED ROLL!"

Friday night and the lights are real bright…

The ride to the city seemed real quick. Couldn't seem to get going and I saw it was bothering the team. They kept asking what's wrong. All I tell them is nothing. I couldn't say I'd been freaking all night, so I just played it as nothing.

It was 6:00 p.m. when we pulled up at Tates Creek High School. The game started at 8:00 p.m. and the parking lot already looked full. Tonight we'd be put to the test I could feel it in the air.

Once off the bus, we walked down to the field to get a feel for it.

Ant walked up. "Yo, bro; I feel like shit."

"Yeah, I know. Your bright ideal wasn't so bright after all."

"Let's just get through tonight and we'll worry about it later."

"Is it me or do those lights seem extra bright?"

"That bitch sucked your senses out. Those lights are the same ones we see every Friday night.

"Switch shields with me."

"I told you about a month ago to get rid of that clear shit alwayz wanting people to see your ugly face."

"Fuck you. Ant, you hating cause I'm pretty and your a slow, white boy."

"Slow, white boy? I may be but I've bailed your black ass out of more jams than I can remember. Pretty? I guess we're running a close race cause I got just as many girls as you have."

"Let's go get ready for pre-game cause I got a feeling it's going to be a long night."

Caged animal…

Bugz hadn't left his apartment since that shit happened yesterday. Two fifths of Wild Turkey later and with a SKS assault rifle at his side, plus a seventeen shot Glock, shit subject to get real ugly fast.

A knock at the door caused him to go to the window. No police cars were in sight but pistol in hand, he answered the door. Goldie was standing there looking straight down the barrel of my nigga's heater.

"Nigga, get that shit out my face!"

"I should blow yo face off, nigga!"

Little did Goldie know how close to death he really was. Now, with a closer look, he saw what the world would soon come to know as the Black Joker; a wild card sho nuff.

"Let's go to the game, nigga."

"Nah, got shit to do."

"Man, clean up and get out this house."

"Where they playing at anyway?"

"Tates Creek. You know there's going to be same bad bitches up there."

"Yeah sho is, give me a few minutes so I can get right."

"I'm a roll some of this good shit so we can get up the road."

"Do that, my nigga; I'll be ready in a minute."

After Bugz went in the back, Goldie breathed a sigh of relief. He knew that nigga was a walking time bomb and he didn't want to be around when he exploded. Goldie, knowing I ain't been home, knew he hadn't told me about the money getting fucked up. It didn't matter either way cause no matter if Bugz fucked up every dollar, I won't care, we'll just go take some more and he knew it so he couldn't wait cause he done fucked up all his money already

The hearts of warriors...

The noise was so loud or maybe I'm tripping. I looked at Ant but I could feel the rest of the team looking at me. What I saw were the eyes of warriors and I knew down inside they would stand strong when I needed them the most.

We made our way to the field. The coin toss was made; we took the ball and we scored first. It looked real easy but boy was I wrong.

Tates Creek scored right back.

After that, things rolled down hill for us. The half time score was 28-7, their way. We made our way to the locker room. I was the last one in with a couple of coaches bringing up the rear.

I heard a voice that made me look up.

"Hey, super star; looks like your having a bad night.

Could you believe Janelle being sassy when a nigga needed a little pick me up?

"Don't worry, smart ass; stick around, my show ain't begun yet."

"Oh, I wouldn't miss it for the world."

With that, she blew me a kiss then turned and disappeared into the crowd.

I had to get this defense together. They were doing whatevea they wanted to. Once in the locker room, I still saw eyes of warriors looking for me to lead so I knew shit would swing our way.

After Coach Mack gave us a speech about having our heads up our asses, we headed back to the field. Me and Ant were the last ones out and Coach T told us to hold up so I knew he was about to chew our asses out. But to my surprise, it was something totally different.

"Boys, don't let me down. I'm a tell ya'll first, this is my last year coaching and I want to go out in style so get ya'll asses in gear."

No answer was given cause we knew somehow, someway we would make the impossible possible. As we were making our way back out to get loose, I hear my nigga Bugz holla.

"Take no prisoners!"

I mumble to myself.

"Leave no one alive."

The fast pace swings are way though the fourth quarter still down four points; we had to get this ball back. Their running the ball straight down are throats. In the huddle I tell Ant.

"Hold that runner up I'm going to strip that ball from him."

"Just hurry up an get up here before he tries to lay down."

I looked at my partner Darnell, a.k.a Flem-Bo. He's really from Louisville but he was in a group home called the Holland House. That nigga was a soldier on this field.

I didn't say nothing cause nothing needed to be said. I could feel a light breeze blowing in my ear hole and for some reason a smile crept across my face. (Later that smile would be known as the smile that would appear right before my body count went up.)

Ant did what I asked but it wasn't me who got the ball. That nigga Flem-Bo was going the other way for six after the extra point 28-31 our way. We had to go right back out on the field with 44 seconds left.

They were going to try to get in field goal range. On their first play, they threw a short pass and got out of bound with the ball on their own 40. The second play, Ant gots a sack; the clock was running and there were no time outs.

We knew they were going deep, but me playing to be the hero, bites on a short pump fake on a hitch route and I got burned bad. That boy was off to the races. I couldn't believe it as I gave chase. I knew I couldn't get him and all I see was the clock hitting zeroes. My teammates helped me save face and you wouldn't believe who bailed me out. That slow-ass, white boy Ant tackled that fool on the three yard line. I fell to my knees. Happy ass, a mutha fucka. We got away again. Damn, I owe these boys big time.

The party after the war…

The bus ride home was like heaven on earth. Couldn't explain the feeling. Everybody was going crazy but I was in my own world. I knew Faye had to work early in the morning so I would just hang out in the hood. I wasn't going back out to Ant's tonight; I wanted to be in my hood. I gave some of the guys some money so they could enjoy themselves then I had

Ant drop me at home. I walked through the door and saw Bell sitting there watching TVG gambling, like alwayz.

"Hi, Bell."

"Boy, you played like pure trash and you didn't even blow me my kiss."

"Yeah, I know things were ruff tonight."

"Nah, you leave that little fast-ass, white girl alone when you go to the country you would be okay."

I don't know how Bell knows everything I do but she was right that girl took it out of me last night.

"I hear you; where's L at?"

"Over Don-Don's house."

"Yeah, well I'm bout to walk down the street so I'll see you later."

"Okay, baby; you be safe down there. It's a little hot since that girl got killed yesterday."

For some reason when she said that I knew who was behind it all without even knowing the story.

Damn, I wonder what happen this time. I guess I'll find out soon enough. Once down the street I saw a couple of cars parked on the curb. As I walked up, it was Bugz and Goldie.

"What's up my niggas?"

"Shit ain't nothing; waiting on you. Here's some drink to relax yourself after you almost gave the game away."

"I can't lie I liked to fucked up in the worst way but that's what them other fools are for."

"Yeah, yo man saved yo ass."

"Yeah, but check this, what's up with this shit Bell just ran by me about some girl getting killed. I got no response so I knew the answer but I didn't press the issue right now but somebody was going to tell me something real soon. Fuck it, lets get ripped right now and worry about that shit later.

After about 30 minutes of kicking it with them fools and a couple more of the homies, this car pulled up loaded with people. I didn't know the car and neither did my people, so we got quiet and a few of them even touched their hips, ready for whatevea. I looked at Bugz and he passed me a pistol on the low. But to my surprise, what I heard was music to my ears.

"What's up, super star?"

Janelle had a funny way of showing up when the time was just right.

"Nelle, what you doing down here? You liked to got shot up pulling up like that."

"You country niggas can relax; we're just trying to have some fun."

"Dig, well ya'll get out and let's have some fun."

Don't get it fucked up; all these broads were nice as hell so I knew my niggas were going to go all out trying to catch one of them. Tonight Janelle wasn't going to get away without giving me some of that pussy. I didn't have to put my press game down cause she put the press on me.

"What's up, country nigga; you think you can handle two or what?"

Now you know that shit really caught me off guard but being a real player, I let that shit roll.

"Why not three?"

"We'll see, Shonda. Aye, Shonda come here for a second, I want you to meet somebody."

"Yeah girl, what's up?"

Shonda was chocolate as a mutha fucka and had ass and titty everywhere. Plus her lips looked like they were wet as hell.

"Remember when I said I wanted to put on a show, well here's the nigga I was talking about."

"Can this nigga handle both of us?"

"That's what I just asked him."

"Well, can you nigga or what?"

"Bitch, bring the whole car load and I'll send all ya'll home with sore pussies."

The smile I got let me know I may have bit off more than I could chew. But fuck it. Ball til you fall.

"You talk tough but when I get my hands on you, we'll see!"

"I guess we will."

She went back over to where everybody else was and Janelle gave me a devilish grin; shit bout to get real interesting.

Detectives working overtime...

After the game, Detective Reeves went back to the office just to get some paper work but got a message off the answering machine. The person said they had information on some robberies and maybe a murder but they didn't leave a name or number but said you might want to talk to Henry Lewis, a.k.a. Bugz. The smile that appeared on his face was like a kid on Christmas. Now he could pick my nigga up on a 72 hour hold but what he would get, would be a total embarrassment in front of his co-worker.

But even that wouldn't be enough to stop him.

"I've got you now, you little black porch monkey."

Party of a lifetime…

I went back up the street to get my car so I could take the girls home in the morning. Once I got back to the park, Janelle and Shonda got in the car with me. Now you know some of my niggas were hot but what can I do if they choice pimping. I got out and went over to Bugz.

"Give me the key to your apartment."

"Yeah, no doubt; I've been meaning to give you your key anyway."

"Why it take you so long?"

"Nigga, you been out there with them white folks plus what you about to do with them two bad bitches?"

"I don't know yet but after I show these other girls how to get back to the highway, I'm going your way."

"Dig, I'll get at you later cause I'm going to shoot same dice at the 447 Club."

"Take yo heater in there; you know them old niggas be tripping when they be losing."

"I know, me and Tea-Cup got into it last time I was there."

"Man, that old nigga is a cowboy; watch that nigga."

"If that nigga gets out of line, I'm a blow his face off."

"All right, my nigga; be safe. I'm gone."

"Nah, nigga. You be safe. That chocolate bitch looks like she's a beast!"

"I'm the beast master."

The laugh we shared was that of life-long friends who would go through hell and high water together. No money or bitch could get between that, *ever*.

After showing Janelle's friends how to get to the highway, I bee-line straight to my niggas house. Once there, shit wasn't no game.

"Ya'll want something to drink or something?"

"Nah, nigga. Don't stall us out. You was running yo mouth a little while ago."

"Ain't no thang; let's go in the back."

After shutting and locking the door to the room I fixed as my own, I turned on the light and boy the surprise was on me. Bugz done put a nice bed and everything in this bitch.

Shonda didn't wait another second. She got naked and so did Janelle. I watched for a second as they crawled in the bed together, kissing and touching each other all over.

They stopped long enough for Janelle to say, "Bring yo country ass over here, superstar and let's have some fun, baby."

As I pulled my shirt over my head, I saw them looking at my waist. It ain't my dick they're looking at – it was the pistol that Bugz gave me early; I forgot I had it. Shit, it was like a piece of me. But no worries, if he gave me one, that meant he had two.

I put it on the dresser. I dropped my pants and boxers at the same time and jumped right in between both of them. Shonda was the first to say something.

"Nelle, I think I'm going to like this nigga."

"I told you but wait til he put that dick up in you."

"Fuck that; I got to taste it first!"

And taste she did. Her tongue worked overtime as Nelle kissed her way down to help. I looked at the ceiling and smiled thinking this was the best shit in the world.

"Shonda, let me taste that dick?"

"Bitch, you should sit on that nigga's face."

"Nah, you come sit on my face with yo fine chocolate self."

With my dick in Janelle's mouth and Shonda on my face, shit I was having the time of my life. We fucked and sucked on each other until the girls said they had enough. That put a smile on my face. Big mouth Shonda can't say shit; I beat that pussy up. I laid down between both of them as they laid their heads on my shoulders. With a kiss on both girl's forehead, I dozed off.

Finding out what happened to the money...

The sun was coming through the blinds. When I looked over, Janelle was the only one still in the bed. I heard some arguing going on, so I jumped up and put my boxers on, grabbed my gun and went out the door to see Shonda and Kay standing face-to-face.

"Bitch, what are you doing in my man's house walking around butt-ass naked?"

"I didn't see you in the bed with Dawg last night, so how is he your man?"

Kay had a stupid look on her face. …

Bugz stood in the doorway, just like me - boxers and pistol in hand, with a smile on his face, looking at Shonda and that fat ass.

"What's up bruh; you have fun last night?"

"Yeah, shit was cool."

By now Janelle was standing naked in the doorway asking, "What's going on, baby?"

"Nothing; just a little misunderstanding, that's all."

Kay looked on in amazement as she saw a second naked woman come out the room.

They saw her look and then they both kissed me on my face then went in the bathroom together.

"You're so nasty, nigga; I hope you catch something!"

"I love you too, Kay."

All I got was the middle finger as she went back in Bugz room and slammed the door.

"Man, what you do with those two bad mutha fuckas, my nigga?"

Before I could answer him, the bathroom door swung open and Shonda said, "He beat this pussy up and that one in there, too," pointing her finger at Nelle as she came out of the bathroom.

"Look, my nigga; I'm going to take them to breakfast, then home. When I get back, we need to handle some business."

"I hear you; I'll be here when you get back."

"Get rid of yo big mouth girl, too!"

"Say no more. I'm take her home when you roll out."

After breakfast and a long talk with the girls about last night, we agreed we'd get together soon.

On my way back home, I zoomed to the mall to get super clean. By the time I got back to Bugz house, he was sitting at the coffee table with all the money on the table and a far off look so I knew shit about to be crazy. To keep him from doing something dumb to make shit right, I smooth it over real fast.

"Don't worry, my nigga; hustling ain't our thing anyway."

"I fucked up but I got your cut, my nigga, plus, you can have half of mine."

"Nah, we in it together so whatevea it is, we'll split it down the middle."

"That's why I'll kill anything moving about you."

"I know, but look, did you do that shit the other day?"

The look I got let me know all I needed to know. That was the first person the Black Joker killed, but it wouldn't be the last one.

"Take your money and spend it wise; I'm going back to the country tonight; I'll be back Sunday night."

"Don't worry, I paid the rent for six months so I'll lay low for awhile."

"Give me that gun you used in that shit the other day and give the rest of that work to Goldie; we out the dope game for now."

After he gave me the one gun, I told him, "Just give me all your guns so I can take them out to the country."

"What the fuck I'm going to have?"

"If you stay home, you won't need one and get that work out of here now!"

We left together. I watched him go one way and I went the other. Little did I know what I did at that time saved my main man a Death Sentence.

Chapter 9

Country boys know how to party!!!

I don't have to call when I'm going out to Ant's house, so I just drove myself down there. By the time I got there, it was 8:00 p.m. so it was dark outside. I pulled up in the driveway just as Ant was coming out the door.

"What's up bro? You're just in time."

"In time for what?"

"I'm going to a field party over to Davey and Little Jay's house!"

"Let me pull my car around back."

"Hurry up so I can go pick up a keg of beer Mikey got waiting for me."

As I pulled around back and parked, Big Ant was standing in the doorway telling me to come in. So I made my way in the house.

"Hey son, you and Ant played like shit but I'm proud of ya'll for finding a way to win."

"Yeah, we played bad but we pulled through."

"Yes, you did but here's the real reason why I called you in here."

"What's on yo mind, Big Ant?"

"This is what's on my mind."

I looked down as Big Ant handed me a snub nose .38. Now I knew I had a stupid look on my face but Big Ant cleared the air real fast.

117

"I know you're going with Anthony to that party, so if one of those red neck hillbillies gets out of line, I want you to shoot first and ask questions later. Don't worry about no trouble cause I'll get you the best lawyer in the state of Kentucky."

"I don't think there's going to any problems."

"I know you boys can handle yourself but I want my boys with a winning chance if shit goes bad. Don't worry, I've already given Anthony one, so ya'll have fun."

"Thanks, Big Ant."

"Don't thank me, just get that shit out ya'll system before next Friday and go out on senior night with a bang."

72 hours of hell, but the dam didn't break...

Bugz was lying back smoking some of that good, waiting on Kay to get back from the store. He got up to use the bathroom. On his way out, the front door opened, but Kay wasn't the only one to walk in. Behind her were both detectives and a couple of uniform officers. First thing through his mind was thank God all the work and guns were gone.

"What the fuck ya'll bitches doing in my house?"

"Don't worry, Mr. Lewis, we got a new home for you in the near future, but tonight, downtown will be your resting place."

"Well let's get there so I can call my lawyer."

Mentioning his lawyer brought instant rage to Detective Reeves' face.

"Why would you need a lawyer if you haven't done nothing wrong?"

Without even looking his way as they cuffed him, he told Kay to call his mom to let her know the business. With a warrant to look around the apartment, they ran though it like a tornado. Good thing he took his money to Ms. Joyce's house earlier that day. That money may have cost us dearly.

The funny thing about the whole situation was what he said on the way out. "Is that pretty little wife of yours still crazy about big, black dicks?"

The laugh that was heard let everybody in the room know that they were dealing with a Looney Tune.

Party til you drop, bro…

Once at the party, shit was off the hook. White girls everywhere; big trucks parked in a big ass circle with a big fire raging in the middle. Kegs of beer were everywhere plus fifth after fifth of Wild Turkey.

A lot of the white guys off the football team and Willie was there.

Willie lives down here. Him and his folks came down here from Pittsburg some years back so they know he's been down in the sticks with them.

I make my way over to where he's at. "Wig D, what's up my nigga?"

With a bad little white chick under his arm and a milk jug full of beer leaning on his truck, Willie replied, "Man what the fuck you doing out here?"

"Had to get away from the hood for a second."

"I feel you but if you need me, let me know," He lifted his shirt a little and showed me a .45.

"I'm straight; me and Ant both got one but you be easy; I'm bout to go back over by Ant's truck."

"All right fam, I'll be here until the sun comes up."

That was the last thing I heard as I made my way back to where Ant was. When I got there, he had plenty of company. Girls were all around his truck pumping beer out of the keg he had.

Amanda was there with all her friends. Damn, I don't want to fuck with her tonight. I wanted to see what one of these other white girls were about.

"Hi Dawg, Ant told me you were down here."

"Yeah, just trying to have fun and see what's happening."

"That's what we do when we have one of these field parties is have fun."

I wouldn't understand the meaning of that statement until later and fun would be an understatement.

Down at the jail...

As they were booking my nigga Bugz in, the Detective was trying to get him to talk to them before his lawyer arrived.

"Look Mr. Lewis, we just want to ask you a couple of questions; nothing to serious."

"I tell you what Detective, if you let me fuck your wife, I'll tell you what you want to hear."

"Fuck you; I'll break your black neck."

"See, you need to share that bitch cause I got what she likes," Bugz said that as he grabbed his dick and shook it at the Detective.

Without thinking, Detective Reeves slapped the shit out of Bugz while he was still cuffed right in from of all the jail staff.

"See, you redneck bitch, that twice you've put your dick beaters on me; the next time is on me."

The look on his face let the whole room know he meant what he said.

Mr. Young, the second shift lieutenant who runs the jail, took Bugz upstairs to one of the cells. The Detective knew he had crossed the line by putting his hands on Bugz in front of all those people, especially Mr. Young who was black. He'll have to find another way to break the case.

The true meaning of a field party!!!

A fifth of Wild Turkey and a couple of jugs of beer later, I didn't know if I was coming or going. As I was laid back in Ant's truck with my eyes half closed, the door opened. I thought it was Amanda but it was Tiffany with a devilish grin on her face. I played half asleep to see how far she would go.

"Dawg, are you awake?"

I lay there faking like a mutha fucka and the truck door opened again, this time it was Amanda.

"Amanda, he's passed out drunk."

"Let's wake him up."

Amanda crawls over the seat so I'm in the middle of the two girls. They started working on my belt and then my pants. Tiffany looked like a kid in a candy store so I knew she was about to eat a nigga up.

Amanda was in such a rush, she couldn't get my pants undone, so I helped.

"I knew you wasn't asleep."

"Nah, just waiting to see what ya'll was going to do."

Damn am I this lucky or what?? To have two freaks going at me again. That's two nights in a row. Pants down and dick out, the girls shared me back in forth like an ice cream cone. The only problem I could see was I heard them arguing over who going to get the nut. Let me tell ya'll something; it made me know you alwayz got to have a white girl in your life, even if it's just on the side.

"Damn Amanda, you've been fucking with him; let me get it first!"

"Okay, Damn!"

Amanda looked at me with those puppy dog eyes and asked, "Are you going to give me some after her?"

"I got you baby; now watch me cum in her mouth."

Man this white girl Tiffany sucked the cum right out of me and kept on sucking for about ten minutes straight until I was ready to bust again.

"Damn, I'm bout to bust again!"

When I said that, Tiffany let up just long enough so Amanda could put her mouth on me. Her first slurp got her some cum shot right in her mouth.

The party was far from over. Each girl rode me until I busted in the other's mouth who wasn't riding.

With the sun on its way up, Ant made his way back to the truck.

"Damn, bro; I'm wasted."

"I fucked myself sober; I'll drive home."

"So shit was mad cool?"

"Hell yeah; shit was straight. But check this, I got a bag full of guns I need you to put up."

"No problem, I'll put them in the loft."

"By the way, do you think we could melt one of them in the wielding shop?

"If it can be melted, then we'll do it as soon as we get there."

"Thanks bro; I wouldn't know what to do without you."

"Told you, I alwayz get your black ass out of trouble."

"That you do, white boy; that you do."

Back to the north...

After me and Ant melted that pistol down and told his dad I was putting some guns in the loft, which made Big Ant happy, I made my way back to town. It wasn't late or too early, so I went by Dre's; its alwayz packed on Sunday. Soon as I walked in everybody looked at me like I was a ghost. Gunnz pulled me to the side.

"What's up with Bugz; they let him out yet?"

The look on my face must have told him I just found out he was locked up. "I've been out in the country since yesterday."

"Man, sorry to have to tell you but they picked him up on a 72 hour hold, talking about some robbery and a murder."

I didn't wait another second. I headed straight for the door. Before I could even close to the door, Bell was on me.

"You think that boy is going to keep his mouth shut."

"Yeah, Bell; he's straight that's my nigga

"I hope so for both of ya'll sake cause ain't no coming back from this one."

What Bell said was the truth. We'd been putting in major work for bout a year straight plus this body. Damn.

"72 hours that means he gets out Monday if everything is straight."

"Yeah, but don't you worry bout him; you just keep on going on like nothing ever happened."

"Yes, ma'am but I can't lie to you Bell; we been in all types of stuff."

"I know baby boy and if you live long enough, ya'll two fools will be in even more stuff."

Most of the night I talked to Faye on the phone cause I couldn't sleep. School was in the morning so I told her to go to bed; I'd see her later. Restless, I walked down stairs and Bell was watching TVG, getting her gamble on. We didn't say nothing to each other. I just sat on the couch next to her and watched her do her thing until I dozed off.

Home from 72 and battle tested…

The wind was really blowing when they let Bugz out early that morning. So being that the jail was right downtown, and the hood was closer than walking to his apartment, he made his way to the hood.

Me, I'm on my way out the door to take L to school. He goes to Georgetown Middle so the way I take is right through town. I zoomed past the park and a couple of old heads were sitting out getting their drink on all ready. I hit the horn and kept it pushing. I turn right on Washington Street and guess who I see? I stopped right in the middle of the street and that black mutha fucka didn't do nothing but smile as he walked toward the car. L jumped out and got in the back. I hit the gas with sense of relief having my nigga in the car.

"You okay, my nigga?"

"Yeah, I'm cool; just a busted lip that's all."

"How the fuck that happen?"

"Punk ass Reeves slapped the shit out of me while I was still cuffed."

"Bitch ass cracker!"

"But check this out; what you do?"

That was far as I let him get cause I knew what was getting ready to come out his mouth. I didn't want L all in our business. So he kept quiet until we dropped L at school.

"Don't worry about those guns; they're put up."

"Man, you must be a psychic but I'm glad as a mutha fucka you took that shit and had me get that work out my house."

"It was time for me to say something; you been on a war path lately."

"I know, but I didn't mean to kill that girl; she was in my business so she had to go."

"I ain't mad at you but from here on out, we saving the murder game for those who really need it."

"I got you, bruh.

I let Bugz drop me off at school so he could keep the car. As soon as I got out of the car, Faye was walking in the building so I holla'd for her.

"Hey baby, wait up."

She turned around and a big smile crossed her face.

"Who you talking to? Me? Sorry, I already got a man."

"That nigga better watch yo fine ass before I steal you."

I wrapped my arms around her and got a nice wet kiss that made my day brighter plus knowing my main man was on the streets.

Friday night senior night, my last home game…

I couldn't see this day four years ago. I'd watched a lot of seniors take this walk, now it was my turn. With Momma, Aunt Mia and Aunt Theta on my arms, I made my way to center field. I wish Bell would've come, too but believe it or not, Bell ain't never seen me play a game; I mean not one time.

Lord willing, I'll go out in real style. But the way these niggas from Louisville (Seneca) were talking, you would have thought Charlie Ward and the Florida State Seminoles just rode into town.

They called all the white guys on our team 'cracker' and anything you could think of. They tried to talk shit to us, but yo hood ain't no harder then mine.

When the game started, we found out talking was all they were good at. Man we dog-walked them niggas. Halftime 42-0.

I stood up and asked for the floor. When I got it, what I said made my boys go nuts.

"Hey ya'll, this is it for most of us. We'll never put this red and white on again. Those ass holes came down to the country talking trash in our house. So, let's bust this clock on these sucker and leave our own mark.

The roar that was heard from our locker room made the whole stadium get quiet.

Travis, this white boy from the county, got to making this noise like a train. And that was what it was - a big red train coming back to the field.

Those boys from the city wouldn't respect where we were from but when we got done with them on this field, they would respect our game.

The game was out of hand. The start of the fourth rolled around; the score was 63-0. I asked if I could go back in to return one more punt and Coach Mack gave me the green light. Before we broke the huddle, I told all the young guys, "Help me get to the end zone one last time."

The look on their faces was pure determination. And boy did they help me in, all the way. I didn't get to do it last week, but I did it tonight. As I rounded the back of the end zone, I spotted the 18 Action News cameras, so I popped my helmet and kissed the lens.

The whole stadium went wild. Fuck the unsportsmanlike conduct I got; I just blew Bell her kiss.

Reality sets in...

The playoffs started the next week and we got a bye; but if they won, they were coming back to town again. Boone County. They rolled over Bryan Station and the hype was through the fucking roof. I'm going to keep it short right here we lost to those hillbillies, 13-10. We cried like babies on that field. For a couple of us, it was off to catch up with the basketball team. For me, basketball season would keep me out of the streets for a little while longer.

Spring, 1997 — time to get back at it...

Spring time was right around the corner and I could feel the heat about to come. Kentucky just lost the National title game to Arizona. Me and

Bugz were sitting around at his apartment just kicking it about a bunch of nothing but I felt him leaning toward some bullshit. And what do you know, here it comes.

"Dawg it's been a while since we busted a move; you think shits cooled off yet?"

"Why you broke or something?"

"Not yet, but my money is getting low."

"I've been thinking, we could run to Lexington or Paris and see what we might luck up on."

"I say Lexington cause there's more to choose from."

"We'll go look at some spots and see what it looks like."

"Sounds like a plan to me, my nigga."

Robbery/homicide unit…

"Hey Cris can you believe that the robberys have just up and stopped?"

"Yeah but I bet their just waiting on it to cool off."

"Could be but I think their done."

"Don't bet your retirement on it something bound to happen."

"It's getting ready to get warm so I guess I'll sit back and watch."

"Watch my ass you need to help me solve these old ones."

The Thursday before the Kentucky Derby…

7:00 a.m. Bell is running around the house all out of control. It's been like this since I can remember. I've been up for awhile so I let her do her thing cause I know she is on her way out the door.

"Telly make sure L gets on the bus."

"Yes ma'am."

Bell stopped dead in her tracks and looked at me with a funny look on her face. "Boy don't do nothing stupid this morning."

"I ain't Bell why you say that?"

"I bet little Henry is waiting on you out side."

She doesn't wait on a response she opens the door and steps out on the front porch. She comes back with Bugz right behind her.

"Sit yo black ass down next to that red nigga so I can let ya'll in on a secret!"

He sat next to me with a real stupid look on his face I just shake my head. This cold killer looks like a scared school kid.

"Ya'll boys had one helluva run so I suggest ya'll give that Billy the kid shit a break."

"We ain't on nothing Bell."

"I can feel something bad is going to happen not today but real soon so please don't do nothing dumb."

We just sat there with a stone face knowing that no matter what she said this morning we were going on a move this morning.

"Telly I'm going to tell you once I won't be coming to see you when your sitting down Eddyville. I'm to old to make that trip but it don't mean I don't love you."

She grabbed her purse and went straight out the door and didn't look back.

"I love you too Bell."

Good luck or bad…

Murder bucket gassed up rolling early in the morning means one thing. 211 in progress. The mission was to go to Lexington but being like a eagle with his head on a swivel Bugz see something that might be sweet. The Farmers Bank that sit right on Main and Broadway right downtown. If shit goes bad we won't have far to go to jail. It's about 50 yards away if that. Nothing was said as I turned right like I'm going to Frankfort but I'm really parking down on Water St. About 5 minutes after 9 so we know there open and ain't too many people in there. We can't put are ski mask down yet we got to wait until we get right to the door. Bugz is the first through the doors so he knows he's going behind the teller cage. In the bank I make my point clear right away.

"Everybody be still I won't say this twice the next time my gun will do the talking."

Nobody moved things were good until the bank manager came backing out the back with his back to us but what he brought out with him would be are downfall. Bugz is right there in the tellers cage so he taps the man on the shoulder and when he turns around and see his few employee with their hands over their heads then his eyes landed on me instantly his hands goes up and a smile comes across my face; the same smile he would try to describe to the police.

'Old man, please don't move since you wasn't in here when I give that order I'll give you your fair chance."

I seen Bugz head disappear but I didn't know were he went.

"What you doing hurry the fuck up so we can go!"

"Bingo!"

I didn't know what that nigga meant until we got to his house. When he reappeared I could see a real stupid smile come across his face.

"Put them cracker in that closet over there."

"Ya'll heard the man; move!"

It was a total of 5 people stuffed in that closet but I didn't care. We made are way out the door but stop short when we saw a Georgetown police car parked across the street. So we pulled our masks up and tucked the pistols away and walk out like nothing ever happen. On are way back to the car some one honked the horn at us when I looked up it was Bell and Ms. Rouie. DAMN.

The real come up…

Back at Bugz apartment with the local news blurring about the early morning robbery. Every time we heard a car door closes we jump up guns in hand ready for war. We haven't counted the money yet cause Kay was there. So I looked at Bugz.

"How long it take to get dressed?"

"I don't know but if I go back there I'm going to put my foot in her ass. Should have her ass in school anyway."

"Go give her some money so she can get the fuck on bout her business."

"Hell nah she needs to hurry the fuck up!"

As Bugz got up to go get Kay she came out the back.

"Bout time what the hell took you so long?"

"It don't matter every time this nigga comes around you be acting like this nigga is GOD or something."

"Bitch you open yo mouth one more time I'm going to break yo jaw."

I know he meant every word he said and she did to so she just stood there looking real stupid so to make matters worst I stuck my tongue out at her. Bugz seen it to but it didn't stop him from keeping his word.

"Fuck you Dawg!"

My nigga moved so quick I didn't have time to stop him. He slapped the shit out of her I know it ain't my place to get in no man business when it comes to his woman but I started it.

"Fam, you didn't have to do that."

"Yeah you right but I told that bitch to keep her mouth shut."

Still on the floor scared to move Bugz finally tells her.

"Get yo ass up and get on out of here."

"You didn't have to hit me like that."

"Well if you would've took yo ass to school this morning like I told you then you wouldn't be here."

"Dawg ain't in school."

"See that's your mutha fucking problem all in grown men's business now take this money and get yo ass to school I'll see you later."

132

She didn't say shit just grab the money and went to the door but she stopped as she open the door.

"Both of ya'll are some punk bitches."

She jumped down a whole flight of stairs after she said that we just laughed.

"Lock that door my nigga and let's count this money."

"Yeah I bet we got 30 or 40 thousand."

"Nah, not that much."

"Fuck it lets see."

We start to count and when we got past 130,000 thousand with more still on the table I looked at Bugz he jumped straight up and grab the SKS and went to the window. I. just keep counting when I was done we had 215,271. Man I ain't never seen this much money. Time to ball. My graduation is in two weeks and I all ready signed my letter with Marshall University. I would be close to home.

Chapter 10

We balled hard…

Saturday, May 9 was my nigga's birthday. We bout to act a fool. The week after Derby and we needed any reason to keep partying on our way to Cincinnati to go shopping. Bank roll was super fat.

"Bugz, you going to be asleep before the party tonight."

"Fuck it. I don't know when I might see another one of these mutha fuckas."

Goldie's in the backseat. He was a little hot with us about not taking him on the move but hell, Bugz gave that nigga 11 zones so he should be straight.

"Let that nigga do him; he'll be straight by tonight."

"Nigga, who asks you anyways?"

"All I'm saying is it's his birthday not yours."

"Whatevea, pass my shit."

We made it to the Nati Smitthy's old ass won't let but 5 people in his store at one time. Old Jew mutha fucka, the only store that made it through the riots. All I wanted out of this bitch was some Chucks.

He got all colors from there we shot to the mall. Last but not least, we go to Alabama's a fish spot in (OTR) one of the meanest hoods in Cincinnati. Show them your I.D. on your birthday and get a free fish sandwich. I got Bell one. She loves that shit.

Back on the highway to make the 71 mile trip back south to Georgetown. The party would be one for the record.

My body count begins…

The party is at Cardome in the basement. It's a spot you can rent going out toward the county.

I knew it was going to be fat up in there but I got to keep my heater close. On my way out, Bell stopped me in my tracks.

"Baby boy, I'm getting old. Wish you would slow down enough to see you got a chance."

"Bell, I'm headed to Huntington in less than 2 months; I'll be okay."

"I know Bugz party is tonight, but do me a favor. Go back upstairs and get a bigger gun than that little-ass .38."

"I'll be cool Bell with what I got. Plus how you know what gun I got?"

"Cause that big pistol makes your back pocket sag more; now, go get it before you leave."

"Yes ma'am."

"Tell those people down in the country I said hello."

Before I could ask her what she meant by that, she headed for her room. Now, what the fuck was that supposed to mean?

Party time…

As I pulled up I saw that it's packed so I park in the back. I drove the murder bucket cause I didn't want to park the 96' in this gravel. I saw Faye's car so I knew I was going to have fun. On my way in, I see this nigga I ain't never seen so I pat my pocket to make sure my burner there.

Once inside, I saw the party was in full swing. I made my way over to where Bugz was at.

"Happy birthday bruh; I can't believe your still standing."

"Can't stop now; shit bout to get good."

"I know that's right but check this, my nigga. I seen some weird looking nigga outside.

"I seen that nigga earlier. I think he's with Jim-Bob and that nigga Ty from Lexington."

"I'm going to keep a close eye on that nigga."

"Fuck that nigga. Enjoy yo'self and try to fuck something."

"Nah. Faye's up in here somewhere."

"Here we go again about that country bitch."

"Man, what I tell you about yo mouth?"

"My fault bruh; just bullshitting, have fun."

And fun was an understatement. We partied to the wee hours, about 3:00 a.m. I went to the murder bucket and I saw this nigga creeping on my nigga Snoop as he was leaving the party.

Feeding time…

Can you believe this nigga trying to rob my nigga? I watched for a second to see his intentions; boy were they bad. I couldn't hear what he said but I could tell Snoop didn't like it. I eased my way around so I was behind them. When I did get close enough, I heard the tail end of what he was saying.

"Yeah, you country niggas getting money down here, I should have been down here taking it from ya'll's asses."

"Man, take that shit and get the fuck on!"

"Shut up punk before I blow yo head off!"

I took all I could take. I eased right up next to that nigga and whispered, "You picked the wrong nigga," right before I blew his brains out.

In one quick motion, Snoop rolled to the ground. When he came up, his pistol was in his hand.

"What the fuck took you so long?"

"I had to get around those cars."

"Well good looking, let's get this nigga in my trunk."

"You think anybody heard that shot?"

"Hell nah, everybody downstairs is fucked up."

"Yeah, but check this. I got the murder bucket parked right here."

"Okay let's hurry up before somebody comes out."

We put that nigga in my trunk. I was about to go inside and get Bugz but I know he would get his chance to see the hogs up close and personal in the future. "What you going to do with him?"

"Don't worry, just go on home; I'll check you later."

"I owe you one, young nigga."

"Ain't nothing; you would have done it for me."

"Sho would my nigga be safe."

"Northside!"

"Northside."

With that, I pulled out of the lot and headed North on U.S. 25 to my destination. I know Ant's about to get up to help with the farm, so I might make it in time. It took me a little while longer to get to Ant's cause I had to drive slow with that body in the trunk. When I pulled up, the lights were on in the house so I knew everybody was awake. Damn. It wasn't long before my car was noticed. Big Ant flashed the porch lights at me, but I didn't move. So after a few minutes he came out of the house.

"You okay, son?"

"Big Ant, I messed up bad."

"Can we fix it or is it too bad?"

"The problem is in the trunk."

"Well it ain't no problem then; did anybody see you do it?"

"No, sir."

I lied, but I trust that nigga.

"Well I'm going to get Anthony. I won't be coming up to the barn, but he'll know what to do."

"Thanks, Big Ant."

"I told you I alwayz wanted my boys with a winning chance so no thanks is needed."

"Yes, sir."

"Pull your car all the way in the barn and make sure you wash your trunk out good."

"Yes, sir."

"One more thing, this is never, I mean never, to be discussed, ever. Do you understand me, Telly?"

"Yes sir."

"All right now get on up to the barn Anthony we'll be on his way."

My first, but not Ant's...

Once in the barn, I turned the lights on. The smell was so bad I almost threw up. Those big old hogs stink something terrible. I could tell they were hungry by the way they were crowding the gate. I'd seen this many times before when I helped at the farm. I heard Ant's truck pull up; he came in all business.

"Pop the trunk, bro."

I popped the trunk and when we looked inside, dude's whole side of his face was missing.

"You weren't playing with this guy."

"That .44 bulldog is a show stopper."

"Let's take care of this so I can lay back down."

We put the guy in the tuft, those hogs went crazy when they smelled that blood. Ant hit the feeder button and felt the tuft half way. After that I pulled the gate open and let them out, damn, they didn't waste no time eating everything in that tuft. The only thing left was the rubber on the bottom of dude's shoes."

"Ant I ain't never seen no shit like that."

"I have. I'm going to tell you this cause I know dad loves you like me and Mikey. A few years back, dad caught this guy growing marijuana on our property. He shot and killed him and we fed him to the hogs. Believe me, dad is no play thing."

"That's why Big Ant said it's not a problem."

"Yeah bro, it ain't and any time this problem appears, we'll make it disappear."

"Saved my black ass again."

"It's becoming a lifelong job."

"Thanks Ant, but what about the gun?"

"We'll melt it later; lets go lay down plus we'll wash the car out later."

"Say no more."

When we got to the house, Big Ant was drinking coffee. I nodded my head and he did the same. Nothing needed to be said cause I knew then I was in the midst of a real killer.

From graduation to the state pen...

I walked across the stage as Mr. Figgs handed me my diploma. My momma was smiling from ear-to-ear. Even Bell was there. I knew the party would be off the chain. I saw Bugz and Goldie, plus Faye was there, too. Afterwards, we went to eat and then to Project Graduation.

Project Graduation is where all the seniors are locked up in the school. I took my nigga Goo cause I knew Cee-Cee was going to take Faye. Music, games and all the food and drinks you could eat. This would be the last time this senior class would be together for one reason or another.

Time to pay the piper…

Kay was pushing Bugz car around not knowing she had $40,000 in the glove box. Smoking weed, riding though downtown and being that it was a little late, the police pulled the car over.

The officer made his way to the driver's side. "Hello, ma'am. One of your tail lights is out."

"Oh I didn't know, officer; I'll get it fixed."

By now he smells the weed, so now shit about to take a turn for the worst.

"Ma'am, have you been smoking marijuana tonight?"

Like a real dumb ass, she says the wrong shit. "Earlier, but I was on my way home."

"Can I search the car, ma'am?"

"Yes, sir."

Once out of the car, she stood to the back. She knows ain't no drugs but that money was in the glove box and still in the bank wrapper. He opened it and I'll be damn if he don't have it in his hand.

"Ma'am, can I ask you were you got all this money?"

"What money, officer?"

"This right here."

When he showed her, she couldn't believe her eyes. All that money was just sitting in the glove box. The first thing out her mouth was our down fall, but she didn't know any better. She was young and scared to death. "That belongs to my boy friend," she said.

"Who's your boy friend ma'am?"

"Bugz."

"Does Bugz have a real name?"

"Yes."

"Well, I'm waiting."

"Henry Lewis."

It took a second for the name to register, but when it did, he jumped right into action.

"Ma'am, can you put your hands behind your back, please?"

"For what? I ain't done nothing."

"For your safety and mine."

After Kay was cuffed, he called for a female officer, then radioed Robbery/Homicide.

"Detective, I may have something you might want to see."

"Okay, I'll meet you at the jail."

"10-4 in route."

Game over...

Kay was at the jail crying her eyes out. They were putting the full court press down on her.

"Call Bugz and tell him what happen."

"No, I can't."

"Well, we're going to charge you with first degree robbery, young lady."

"For what; I didn't do nothing."

"We'll see. Since you have $40,000 and the serial numbers match the ones from the robbery at the Farmers Bank, it's all on you. You're looking at 20 easy."

Once they throw that number out there she broke.

"Give me the phone."

"You're doing the right thing, young lady."

"Man fuck ya'll!"

The smiles on their faces would be ones to remember.

After a couple of rings Bugz picks up the phone half sleep, "Yeah."

"Bugz, they got me at the jail talking about I robbed a bank."

"What the fuck you talking bout?"

"I got pulled over in your car and they found $40,000."

Damn was all he could say. He was supposed to have put that money up, now he was stuck. If he goes down to the jail, it's over. But he loved that girl so it didn't take long to answer, "Sit tight baby, I'm on my way."

Slipper count in this game…

When I got home and heard the news, I scrambled to clean up the house. I couldn't go far, so I hid my guns down in the grave yard behind our projects. I gave my money to Aunt Mia.

As soon as she left, half the police force was on Teddy Avenue. Damn, we had a good run.

After they cuffed me, Bell said with tears in her eyes, "Baby, granny is tired but know I'll alwayz love you."

"I love you, Bell."

"You was a man when you were doing wrong; be one when they give you what you got coming."

"Yes ma'am."

They rushed me to a waiting car. By the time I got to the jail, news cameras were everywhere. Once inside the jail, I asked for a lawyer, so they went on and took me upstairs. They put me in 217, the lock down cell, with the Federal inmates.

Phat Man was in there watching the news shaking his head.

"Damn, young nigga; ya'll was tearing they ass up."

"Yeah, but the run is over."

"Did you see Bugz yet?"

"Nah, got him around on the high side in 245."

"Don't trip, little bruh; that bank wasn't FDIC funded."

"What the fuck's that mean?"

"Mean the Feds won't pick ya'll case up."

"Damn, I didn't know one way or the other until now. Think I can beat it?"

"Going to be hard with a confession and a surveillance video."

"Damn!"

"They said on the news that you couldn't see the suspect that is by the door."

"What's that mean, Phats."

"Peep this, you never see the person behind the cage with no gun and they never saw suspect number two at all. If anything, it's second degree not first degree. No weapon. If all else fails, get your lawyer to argue that in a plea deal."

"Thanks for the run down, big dogg.

"Keep yo head up, my nigga; you'll be all right."

"No doubt."

The C.O. hollered lock down so I went in my cell with this weird-ass nigga from Lexington. The Feds got this nigga when they raided this nigga house - he was asleep in a coffin; shit already getting crazy.

LaGrange to Eddyville...

We got it broke down to second degree. I was going to go to trail but the detective pulled some bullshit on Bugz. So I took my lick 10 years two to the parole board. But I'm filing for shock.

They wasted no time getting us to the Roddeer Correctional Complex (a.k.a The Fish Tank). This place was an animal house. Young niggas everywhere with all day. They put me in Block 2, G-Unit. Sixty-four niggas waiting to get classified. Bugz was in the same block but a different unit.

They asked you where you wanted to go, so I told them, "Blackburn, Frankfort, or Marion County."

That cracker laughed in my face.

"Well son, you have 34 points. Only one place for you - Eddyville Kentucky State Penitentiary."

"How far is that from Georgetown?"

"About 5 hours."

"Damn!"

"Good luck young man next."

On my way back to the unit I see Bugz. "What's up bruh? Where they sending you."

"Luther Luckett."

"Damn bruh, they sending me to the castle."

"Eddyville, damn don't trip; we got a couple of O.G's down there."

"I don't know them old niggas."

"We'll get to know them niggas and stay low."

"Lock down. All inmates report to your wings!"

"Dawg, don't forget you got 90 days to file for shock. You got a good chance, so make sure you call home and keep your people on it."

"Tru, my nigga; take care. I'll see you in the world."

"You, too. Ain't no thang, baby boy."

We part ways. This would be the last time I saw this nigga for five years. One of us would be locked up and the other one would be free.

Chapter 11

Eddyville to home, but my Bell was gone…

The morning we left the fish tank, all I saw was old convicts shackled and black boxed. I'd met a few of them, all old stick-up men and killers. No one talked on the three hour bus ride to the sticks of Western Kentucky.

The first time I saw the castle I said to myself, "What the fuck have I got myself in to."

It was raining and real fucked up outside; nothing but water around this bitch. Now I see why they call it The Castle on the Cumberland. We roll in the wall is so high, you damn near break your neck looking up. Gun towers manned by KKK-looking mutha fuckas who can't wait to put a bullet in yo ass. We go to the clothing house to get our bed roll and uniforms then to your cellblock. Me, I went to A Block. Everybody's got a cell by themselves, so that was cool. I put my stuff up and sat on my bed. Some big old nigga came to my cell. I ain't never seen this nigga before a day in my life but I knew this nigga was somebody cause he called me by my dad's name.

"Little Carl, you okay?"

I looked at this nigga like he was stupid.

"Man, when I left the streets you were still sitting on yo momma's lap drinking milk. I'm Hicks, Jr."

"Damn, what you been gone about 15 or 16 years now?"

"Something like that little brother but we know you was coming way before you got down here. I'll take you to meet Blakemore later but here same goodies to hold you off."

"Man, I'm straight I got my stuff from the tank."

"Look little brother, I ain't going to get in your business but don't lie down and give up; stay on that lawyer's ass and file for anything you can get."

"I'm on top of that."

"Okay, baby boy; I'm on the second tier if you need me."

"Digg, I'm going to get settled in; I'll get at you later."

One month at the castle…

I've been waiting on the shock probation to go through. I haven't called home in about a week. So I made my way to phones. After waiting 15 minutes, I got a phone. I was going to call Bell first. The phone rang about six times before someone picked up.

"Hello."

"Who's this?"

"It's your Aunt Theta's boy."

"Oh hi, how you doing?"

"I'm fine and you?"

"Doing the best I can do; where's Bell?"

There was a long silence on the phone, so I asked the question again.

"Where's Bell at?"

"Telly, I don't know how to tell you this but Bell passed away two days ago."

"Don't play with me; now put Bell on the phone!"

"Hold on, baby; here's yor momma."

"Hey baby boy how you doing?"

"I'm fine now where's Bell?"

"Baby Bell is gone."

"No, no, no, momma; how could she die before I get home?"

"Baby, you got to stay focused and pray so you can come home."

"Momma, I'll call you later."

I heard her say, "I love you."

But I was so numb, I didn't know if I was coming or going. I went to my cell and cried like a baby; my granny was gone. The next couple of weeks were a blur. They came all the way to Eddyville to transport me back so I could see the judge about my shock probation. On the long ride back to the county jail, my mind was on Bell. It didn't matter too much one way or the other about getting out; my heart was already gone. They put me back in lock down with Phat Man. So we kicked it little bit.

"Lil Bruh, how you holding up down there?"

"Ain't nothing; seen a couple of the old homies from the hood but shit got me fucked up about Bell."

"Yeah, I'm sorry bout yo lost but you got to keep it pushing."

"I got court in the morning so I'll know the out come then but peep this were they send Derrick?"

"Up to the USP in Lewisburg."

"Damn, they going hard up there."

"He's straight; he's at the boot camp."

"Digg, what they going to do with you?"

"I hope Lexington or Manchester."

"Yeah, my nigga; I'm in Kentucky, but shit I'm 5 hours away."

"But you got a chance to make a break tomorrow."

"I hope so."

"You'll be straight now let's make something to eat."

Man I couldn't eat if I wanted to but I sat up with Phat Man until lock down. In a cell by myself, sleep would be little and my thoughts would run wild.

Back to the streets, ASAP…

Nine a.m. when I walked in the court room; it was packed; everybody - family, friends, Big Ant and somebody whose smile caught me by surprise. She's from the hood but I wonder who she's down here to see. It don't matter now, my freedom is at stake. They seat me and there're bailiffs all over the place.

As the judge enters the court room, all became quiet. He starts the proceeding with a quiet conversation with my lawyers and the D.A. They talk for about five minutes I turn around and look at my momma; she smiles and blows kisses. But I got to look a little further to the back. I wanted to see if she is still back there. I'll be damn, she was still there. She smiled and waved if I make it up out of here I'm going to see what's on her mind. Big Ant winked; that gave me a good feeling. The judge hit his gavel and said all rise.

"Mr. Shyne, I don't know why the D.A would recommend this, but somebody must have really got in his ear. So I'm going to grant you shock today, but you better make us all proud. You should be able to get a late entry into somebody's school."

I turned around to look for Big Ant but he was already gone. So I know he was behind me getting out. I step to the microphone, "I won't your honor."

"You have to go back to the prison to be released. Bailiff, please start the process of the transport so he can be released. The paper work will be faxed down there and will be waiting on you Good luck Mr. Shyne."

They take me to the jail but I wasn't there long but I got to holla at Phat Man before I left.

"We know you made it before you even got back."

"Damn I hope shit a go when I get back down there."

"Don't trip baby boy just make sure you make it work for the best."

"Man, you know momma's address; holla at me when you touch were ever you're going so I can send you a bank roll."

"Bet that; hold yo head high, the streets are watching."

"Shyne B and B lets roll."

"That's my ride, my nigga."

"Take that ride to the moon then jump off on one of them stars and shyne."

With that we hugged and dapped it would be years before I saw Phat Man. The ride back to the castle was quick. As soon as I got there, they told me to pack my shit. I gave what I could to my homies then went to the clothing house. After that, they walked me to this big steel door and let me out. When I looked up at the gun tower, this cracker pointed his finger at me like he had a gun and pulled the trigger. Red neck bitch; fuck it, I'm out.

No lights but Saturday afternoon is just fine...

My brother and my home boy, Moo-Coo, came and got me. They brought new clothes but my mind was on other things. Once back home, I stayed at Bell's with my Aunt Theta.

"Baby Boy, you know they going to make us move."

"Yeah, I know but I had to stay here for some reason."

"Just wanted to let you know; I'll see you later."

"Be safe I'm going to chill for a minute."

After my Aunt left I called Faye she couldn't believe I was home. Said she was on her way over but I stopped her.

"Nah baby, my head all fucked up right now; still got Bell on my mind."

"Okay baby, I don't care what you say I'll be over tomorrow."

"Digg, I'll be waiting."

"I love you!"

"Yeah, I know."

I just lied to Faye. I got that smile that I seen at court today on my mind so I had to go out and see if I could get up with her. Thick, young ass got me fucked up right now, but not for long.

Found my prize…

I walked down the street. Everybody was out; it's summer time. And it's only 8:30p.m. A few of my old partners hollered at me but I kept it moving. Got to find what I was looking for. I walked over to the front side of the park BINGO.

"Hey Randi, can I holla at you for a minute?"

Like a shy school girl, head down sucking on her thumb; shit was too cute. We walked away from everybody.

"Hold yo head up baby; I won't bite you."

"Telly, you so silly; I know you won't bite, but I just might."

"Okay, that's cool. I'm with that, but I got to know what was you doing in court today?"

"Wanted to see if my childhood crush was going to get out."

"Oh yeah? What time you got to be home."

"I'm down here with my sister but we're going back to Lexington later on."

"Go tell her you'll be up on Teddy."

I watched her walk over to her sister. They were talking then she looked at me with a silly smile on her face. They walked over to me her sister said, "Boy, you in trouble; you don't know the half of it."

"That trouble ain't so bad plus I'm a big boy."

155

"I'll be to get her about 1:00 a.m. so have her ready."

"Just hit the horn."

She didn't say shit, just walked off sucking her thumb like her sister.

"Randi, you cool with this?"

"Boy please, I'm bout to show you something."

"Yeah, it's a show I can't wait to see."

Big ass, big titty; a young niggas dream...

Once we were back at my house, we went upstairs. She seemed a little scared, so I told her to relax.

"Put on some music," she asked.

I put in my Guy CD and went to my favorite song *'Piece of my Love'* she came straight in my arms.

We started kissing and hugging.

"Turn off the lights."

"Hell nah, I want to see this."

She started undressing. Damn, she was thick, I mean real thick. My dick was rock hard. I jumped out my clothes as fast as I could and walked over to her. She had to get up on her toes to kiss me.

"Lay down baby, I got to get in this pussy."

"Take yo time baby."

I started to lick that pussy but she stopped me.

"I'm already wet. Just seeing you makes my pussy get wet."

To prove a point, she rubbed her fingers across her pussy then stuck them in my mouth I leaned straight in and kissed the shit out of her. I don't know how it happened, but I was in the pussy. Boy, shit was hot as a mutha fucka. She was biting and licking all over me and had me in another world. She said in between breaths, "Turn me over and hit it from the back."

As I turned her over, my dick got even harder looking at all that ass. She looked over her shoulder with that same smile I'd seen earlier today.

"Put it back in, baby."

When I slid back up in that pussy, I lost my mind. Watching that ass move back and forth was more then I could take. But what took the show was when she reached back under herself and rubbed my nuts. That was it! I pulled out and nutted everywhere. We didn't stop there. She stood up and grabbed her ankles; I hit it like that until I busted again. We took a light break trying to catch our wind but ended up dozing off. When I looked at the clock, it was 12:45 a.m. I tapped her on her shoulder; she was slow about moving.

"Baby girl, yo sister will be here in a minute."

"Yeah I know; wish I could stay with you."

"Don't trip baby; this ain't the last time we do this."

"I hope not."

Randi got up and went to the bathroom. By the time she got back, I heard a horn blowing. As we headed back downstairs, she stopped half way down.

"You know I've been in love with you since I can remember."

"Don't trip; your love is safe with me."

I kissed her on her big, soft lips once at the door. I knew I would go back down the street to see what's going on. You know what they say - old habits die hard.

"Baby girl, let me give you my mom's number cause I'll be moving up on Chambers Avenue with her. So you let me know when ya'll coming back down so I can make some time for you."

"If it's just a little time with you I'll take whatevea I can get."

From what she just said I knew she would alwayz have a special spot in my heart. By this time, her sister had the window down so you know she's bout to run her big mouth.

"Girl, let that nigga go. He'll be here when we come back; you know momma's going to be tripping."

"Okay I'll see you soon, Telly; real soon."

"No doubt baby girl; soon won't be soon enough."

She got in the car and they left. I didn't have a pistol so I felt naked walking down the street. It was my first day home I'll check on that and about maybe getting into school.

Heading to the state capital…

Once settled at my mom's house, I started working out hoping I would get a call soon. A few days went by and I was sitting on the front porch when this car pulled up. I'd seen this guy before just couldn't put the face and the place together.

"Hello young man. You're just the person I'm looking for."

"Do I know you?"

"No not really cause when I was recruiting you, you had your eyes elsewhere."

Now I know who this guy is Kentucky State Head Football Coach.

"Well as you can see, my eyes are right here with nothing to do."

"I hoped you say that; I got plenty for you to do."

"I passed all the tests I needed so what's next?"

"Pack your bags son; we're headed to the state capital."

After telling my mom I was going to school, she was so excited. Told me don't worry bout Nothing.

"What you think about what I'm about to do?"

"I think it's great baby; Bell would've been proud."

"I know; I miss her bad."

"Yeah, baby. Me too. But look, your brother said don't go down there acting like no fool."

"I ain't; where's he at anyway?"

"Work so get your stuff together and get on down that road."

"All right, baby; I love you."

"Love you too, baby."

Chapter 12

Beautiful black women and football...

Once on campus what I saw was amazing. If you have not been on a historically black college or university campus, put it on your to do list. Beautiful, I mean beautiful, black women; all colors, sizes and shapes. My roommate was the starting nose tackle a big ole nigga from Memphis Tennessee.

"Boy, pick yo mouth up off the floor."

"Man these some bad mutha fucka."

"Nah mane, you ain't seen the upper classmen yet."

"It gets better than this?"

"Hell yeah, way better; you'll see in a couple of days."

"I can't wait; I'm a knock me one of these bitches."

"Why just one? If you're like they say you are, you'll have your way down here."

I didn't understand what he was talking about until about 3 games into the season.

Can't stay away from home...

After the first game, I went home that night. Playing on Saturday is a lot different from Friday night. I did get plenty of action. We won 24-10 over Lane College out of Jackson Tennessee. Back at mom's house, I saw

I had a letter from Bugz. Damn this the first time I'd heard from this nigga. I sat down in the living room to read it.

> Dawg,
>
> What up my nigga? I hope you're all right. I heard your playing ball at K-State. It's better than nothing. Me I'm pumping iron and working on my case. They denied me shock said in the hearing I was involved in a lot more stuff they couldn't get us on. So you know Judge Overstreet wasn't trying to hear shit. I go up for parole in 99' maybe they'll show me a little love if I get my GED. But if not I'll keep pulling this bit. I ain't going to hold you up to long just wanted to let you know I'm still in your corner. Take care, my nigga.
>
> ONE LOVE,
>
> Bugz
>
> P.S. Take no prisoners!!

Northside...

"Leave no one alive."

After reading that letter I stepped out on the porch to get some air. And I be damn if Charlene wasn't hanging out her window. Now Charlene, that's my girl. She real old school; if she ain't cussing you out, she don't fuck with you.

"Hey you little punk-ass nigga boy."

"What's up, Beamer?"

That's her nick name to those she fucks with.

"I thought yo little bad ass was suppose to be in school."

"I came home to see what momma cooked, but they went out to eat."

"Well, bring yo ugly ass over here; I made hamburgers and gravy with fried potatoes."

Let me put you up on Charlene's cooking; anytime I get a chance, I want whatevea she cooks.

"You ain't got to tell me twice; let me lock this door."

After I get in Beamer's, I see Vicki sitting in the chair. I know she's bout to start talking shit.

"Hey, nappy-head boy!"

"What's up, Louise?"

"Ain't nothing; sitting in here listening to Charlene holla up and down the street."

Charlene was in the kitchen fixing me a plate but was ear hustling all at the same time. "Don't worry bout what I'm doing in my house, bitch!"

"Shut on up and fix this boy's plate."

"Whatevea; take yo ass to the store and get us some cigarettes."

"Give me some money; I'm a go to Dre's."

"Dawg, give her some money so I can get my lungs out the street."

It ain't never been no problem, me looking out for her, cause she lets me stash my guns, and sometimes myself, at her place. Nobody would know I was laid up in the back of the house but her.

"You want something to drink."

"Hell yeah; bring me a Gordon's gin."

I give Vicki a $50 bill and leaned over and whispered in her ear, "Get her a couple of packs of squares and a couple of gins; bring me two Country Clubs and get yo self something."

"Thanks baby boy that's why you get so much love in the streets."

She grabs her purse and makes her way out the door. Beamer comes back in the room with my plate.

"Here boy; is that enough?"

"Yeah, baby; that's cool."

"Hope she hurries; I need a smoke."

Without a moments delay, she was right back in the window I sat back and enjoyed the food before me. I don't know who she was talking to, but they were getting the business. So, to get her to leave whoever she was cussing out alone, I said, "Beamer, I got a letter from Bugz."

"What that black bitch talking about?"

"Nothing working out and waiting on his turn."

"When he go up for parole?"

"He got awhile but not too long."

Before she could say something else, Saint was hanging in the window talking sweet to her. She was about to start cussing but when she turned around and saw Saint, she softened right up. She called him, "Hey Romeo?"

"What's up, Charlene?"

"Ain't nothing honey, baby, love; just feeding this ugly-ass boy."

"I see he got a big ole plate; what's up young nigga?"

"Ain't nothing eating waiting on Louise to get back with my drinks."

"Here she go right here."

"Yeah what time you going down Dre's?"

"In a minute after Rodriguez comes back around the corner."

"Man, I'm going to roll with you."

Ten minutes went by. I finished eating and was drinking on my beer talking shit with Charlene and Vicki when Saint started hollering for me.

"Beamer, thanks for the meal, baby; you alwayz on time when I need you."

"You know it ain't no problem with me feeding you."

"Yeah, I know; but thanks anyway."

"All right baby, you be safe."

As I hit the door, she holla's after me and Saint.

"Don't you and Romeo be down there in no shit; ya'll hear me."

We walk off laughing cause she went right back to hanging out that window.

That smile got my attention again…

When we get to the bottom, it was packed. I sat outside bullshitting with Mailman and Goldie, I got my back to the door. But when those two nigga quit talking, I turned around and saw Randi standing in the doorway. I waited for her to come out. When she did, she didn't say one word; she just slid right in my arms. I looked at these two niggas and wouldn't you know both those clowns had a smile on their faces.

"Come on baby. I hear my shit playing."

I led her back inside. Guys playing with my drink in my hand and her wrapped around me; shit seems right but it ain't my nigga is behind that fence. I bullshit for a little while longer, but I got to get her alone.

"You staying with me tonight or what?"

"Yeah, that was my plan soon as I saw you."

"You drive down here?"

"I brought momma down here but ain't no thang. You just go with me when I take her home."

"That's cool. I'll be outside when you're ready."

"Okay, baby. I'm a see if she ready to go."

"Nah, don't do that. She'll let you know when she's ready. Let her enjoy herself; I ain't going nowhere."

"Okay, you want another beer?"

"Yeah bring it to me."

I go back outside to fuck with some of the homies. 'Bout 10 minutes later, she brings me my beer. After handing it to me, she leans in and kisses me with a whisper only I could hear.

"I love you."

Before I could say anything she was headed back in. Goldie the first one to say something, "Damn playboy, hook me up with her sister."

"Nigga, what's wrong with yo mouth?"

"I'm just saying, be easy if you'd put in a word for me."

"Yeah, all right pass that bottle; it's going to be a long night. I can feel it."

A lesson on life from Charlene I'll never forget...

Man, last night me and Randi were all over each other. I couldn't get enough of her. On her way to drop me off at my mom's house, she had Mary J. *Share My World* CD playing. I knew then I had to have her in my world for a long time. We pulled up at the house. I saw Charlene still hanging out the window I can tell she been up all night and feeling real good about herself so I know shit is going to get real good any second now.

"Baby girl, where's this leading to?"

"I don't know but I already told you how I felt."

"That's cool but you know I'm in school and a lot of shit happens at school plus Faye is still in my life."

"I'm not tripping on none of that cause in due time all that shit will take a backseat to me."

"Okay baby, didn't want you in the dark but you be careful; I'll see you soon."

"Love you; alwayz have, alwayz will."

I got out the car but I still had the door open so I know she heard Charlene.

"Hey you little ugly bitch been out whoring all night!"

"I've been chilling Beamer what you still doing up anyway?"

"I'll ask the questions now what you doing with that baby? Hey honey, you should stay away from this fool-ass nigga!"

All Randi did was smile but Charlene was far from done.

"Dumb ass broad, just smiling; got another one under your spell."

"Damn Beamer, you doing major hating early morning."

"Well peep this playboy, that little country girl been by here and left a note on your car but I had Vicki take it off; I got it right here."

I leaned back in the car to say goodbye, but I didn't see the smile I was used to seeing. "I'll get at you later."

I got no response so I shut the door and she pulled off with Charlene waving and me thinking about what she just said about not tripping. Females have a funny way of letting their feelings show at the wrong time.

"Charlene, why you do that?"

Using her real name made her look at me a little closer but I knew I had no win coming and what she said next would stick with me for the rest of my life.

"Look little red nigga you don't need to be playing with those young girls' emotions cause it's a mutha fucka when somebody plays with yours. Even though niggas like yourself don't fall victim to emotions, be careful cause I don't want to hear your little punk ass crying to me."

"I ain't playing with nobody's emotions and I bet you read my note."

"No I didn't, ugly boy."

"Yes she did, baby boy!"

That's Louise hollering from inside the house.

"So what's it say then?"

"Why did you come home and not go see her."

"Shit, I should have kept my ass at school."

"Nah playboy, don't cry now; tighten up yo game."

"Whatevea, I'm bout to go back to school. I'll see you after homecoming weekend."

"All right love; be safe down in the capital."

"Next time I come home, please stay out my business."

"You ain't got no business, you little bitch; I run this street."

I smile a cool-aid smile as I got in my car. It don't matter what she does, that's my girl. I pulled off with the window down.

"I love you Beamer."

"I love you too honey, baby, love!"

Black college homecoming...

Homecoming and Albany State was coming to town. Niggas from all over would be in the capital tonight after the game. Win or lose, the party would be the highlight of the day. The Hot Boyz were in town to do the show. I'd been moving around campus like a star. The girls had been choosing real well; got me a chick from Cincinnati and one from a small town in Kentucky called Madisonville. But it was all fun to me. Charlene said something that I would alwayz remember - Don't play with people's emotions cause it ain't no fun when they play with yours. I would learn that the hard way. We lost the game 21-17. But I was looking forward to the party. After a shower and a change of clothes, I headed for the dorms but I'm short stopped by my homies Snoop, Goldie and Jim-Bob.

"What fuck ya'll doing down here?"

"What the fuck you mean we can't let you knock the whole campus off by yourself? So, we came to help you, my nigga."

"In that case you should have brought the whole hood," Snoop said.

"Yeah, I know but let's go to the party. I'm supposed to meet Black Dale there; said he had some fire."

Black Dale was from down this way; got a little of this and a little of that. Word was he's getting real money; wish Bugz was home, we would put that nigga in trunk, damn.

"Let's roll before campus police get to tripping."

The concert was live and everybody was having a good time. We acted a fool til the sun came up. One to remember school was going well up until this point but you heard things around campus and what I was hearing might be a sweet lick. The word I got was it's some Chicago niggas down here hustling real well. The season is about over so I'll look into that real soon.

Old habits die hard...

Season over the holidays rolled around I spent it with my family and Faye. I got to make some time for Randi. We'd been kicking it tough; she even came down to Frankfort but had to be careful cause Faye pops up down there, too. Got a card from Bugz; he's doing fine, got to send him a bank roll. I'd seen something that I couldn't keep passing up. Those

Chi-Town niggas moved around on campus and you could tell they were getting money, so I got to look into getting some fire power. I'm not into robbing niggas, but they were high siding and flashing real swell; might as well get them before those people do.

Spring time 1998...

I ran into a couple of old friends from school and some I knew in passing. Flem-Bo was back in Louisville so I asked him "What it look like down there? Got room for one more?"

"Not really. Me and the twins are fucking them up bad but there's some niggas out of Lexington up there putting in some major work."

"Yeah I heard. Spoony and Los'em them niggas wild as hell."

"So what you trying to do? Come up there by yo self?"

"Nah my nigga but I ain't done shit since Bugz got jammed. I can't keep letting the Chi-town niggas keep running around down here like it's that sweet."

"Give me the word and we'll be down this mutha fucka tonight."

"Hell, nah. I heard about the twins; they too wild. Especially Big D with his trigger-happy ass."

"Well here's a number you can reach me at if you need me."

"True shit my nigga bout to get back to school for spring ball I'll get at you."

"You do that."

"Be safe, my nigga; I'll holla if I need ya'll."

With that Flem-Bo was back on I-64 West back to The Ville. Ain't no way I'd let them wild-ass city niggas come down on my lick. I was already strapped; had the Mac-11 under the seat. I'm getting these niggas tonight. After I told mom, I was gone. I hollered at a couple of the old school cats for a second. The sun was going down so I hopped on I-64 West and headed back to Frankfort. Once on the highway, I fired up a blunt of that good. Damn, big mistake. I exited the highway and as soon as I got off, this state trooper gets right behind me. I had thrown the blunt out but I still had the windows up, so I let them down, but it didn't help. He hit the lights on me. I pulled to the side; the only thing on my mind was the Mac-11 under the seat.

"Good evening, sir. The reason I pulled you over is your tint is too dark."

By now he smelled the weed - I saw the look on his face.

"Have you been smoking marijuana tonight?"

"No sir."

"Well I smell it so could you please step out the car."

"Why? I haven't done nothing."

"But I need you to step out now sir."

I got out the car and he hand cuffed me and stood me back by his car. After a few minutes, he walked back to me with the Mac-11 in his hand and placed me under arrest. No sense in crying Bell always said, be a man and take what you got coming.

I can't help you on this one, son…

Big Ant came down to the jail but the talk was short and sweet.

"Can't help you on this one son the FEDS are on their way in. The word I get is they wish they could get you on some more serious charges."

"I messed up bad this time."

"You'll be okay son; call if you need something."

Now I knew I was in trouble. I was in the county in Frankfort for about a month then I got my wakeup call that the FEDS picked my case up. Charged me with 922.G convicted felon in possession of a firearm is what my lawyer said.

"There's no way around this."

"What's the plea?"

"Well son, the minimum is 60 months."

"Ah hell, that's 12 months to the parole board; that ain't shit."

"No, no, no son. This ain't the state that will be 85% then go home. Well, in your case, back to the state for violation of your release."

"Damn, I fucked up this time."

"Yes you did but not as bad as some, so sign this deal and plead guilty next week and you can get on with your life.

I signed the deal not knowing I would lose six years of my life. But it wouldn't be enough to stop me from trying the streets again but in a much bigger way. Next stop for me, UNITED STATES PENITENTIARY TERRE HAUTE INDIANA…

THE END

Coming soon

from

POD-1 PRODUCTIONS

Kash'd Out The Bluegrass Story Part 2

Let's Get Even The Bluegrass Story Part 3

Chasing The Gingerbread Man

ABOUT THE AUTHOR

I have no regrets about this life I've lived. No wishes to do it over. No crying about all the time I've done and have yet to do. Life is short but there is nothing I've yet to do on those streets that so many young hustla's are chasing.

My heart goes out to all my young nigga's running wild.

Me, there is only one thing that I don't want to do – and that's growing old and lonely and dying in one of these hell holes.

Thanks to all who smiled on this and a real special thanks to all who hated on this. It don't stop till the casket drops.

17603732R00099

Made in the USA
Charleston, SC
19 February 2013